Shemerelda

Also by Peter Tinniswood

A TOUCH OF DANIEL
MOG
I DIDN'T KNOW YOU CARED
THE STIRK OF STIRK
EXCEPT YOU'RE A BIRD

Shemerelda

By The
Incredibly Beautiful
H.H. Washbrook
as told to
PETER TINNISWOOD

HODDER AND STOUGHTON
LONDON SYDNEY AUCKLAND TORONTO

British Library Cataloguing in Publication Data

Tinniswood, Peter
Shemerelda
I. Title
823'.914 [F] PR 6070.I5S/

ISBN 0 340 22718 4

 Printed in Great Britain for Hodder and Stoughton Limited, Mill Road, Dunton Green, Sevenoaks, Kent by St Edmundsbury Press, Bury St Edmunds, Suffolk. Photoset by Rowland Phototypesetting Limited, Bury St Edmunds, Suffolk. Hodder and Stoughton Editorial Office: 47 Bedford Square, London WC1B 3DP.

For Kate

'This looks interesting'

introduction

I have been asked to explain the nature of my involvement with the incredibly beautiful H. H. Washbrook.

I have been asked why I, distinguished author, playwright and journalist in my own right, should have agreed to be the Boswell to his Johnson.

I have been asked by countless desirable and ravishing young women for the home address and telephone number of the incredibly beautiful H. H. Washbrook.

Questions, questions, questions.

Mind your own business!

chapter one

Shemerelda, rich and beautiful, drew back the languid morning curtains.

The green lawns of the mansion loped down to the white Atlantic strand.

Sea birds mewed and creaked.

A jet plane spat silver at the sun.

Shemerelda felt nervous and excited.

She knew her life was about to change.

Shemerelda, rich and beautiful and young as well, lived in a mansion on the southernmost tip of the island that holds Rackham City.

Rackham City is in the USA.

Oh yes it is.

Look on your maps.

chapter two

At breakfast that morning Shemerelda's husband, Leonard, said:

"I hope you slept well last night, Shemerelda."

Shemerelda said:

"Yes, I did, thank you, Leonard. I hope you, too, slept well."

Leonard smiled at her.

A damp smile.

"Thank you, my dear, I did," he said.

Ahah!

chapter three

The Tozer tree in the lower gardens of the mansion bloomed twice a year.

In the spring its flowers hung deep and scarlet and murmured softly to themselves at night.

In the fall the flowers were jet black.

It was springtime now and Shemerelda stood beneath the spreading boughs of the Tozer tree.

She reached up and plucked a deep and scarlet bloom.

She put her mouth silkily inside its gape and whispered:

"Tell me, tell me. Will I fall in love tonight?"

She held the bloom at arms length and pursed her lips in a kiss.

Then she placed it to her ear and listened intently.

She thought she heard these words:

"Yes, Shemerelda. Yes, you will."

But she could not be sure.

Leonard arrived home early from work that day.

He was a banker.

In the evening there was to be a party in his home.

His parties were sumptuous and invitations were dearly prized.

The mansion was decked en fête.

Myriads of fairy lights sparkled on its roof and its vine-encrusted walls.

Siam-scroll lanterns hung from the trees and bushes in its gardens.

Braziers of sweet-scented sandalwood burned in its arbors and in its bowers.

And the deep-bellied Atlantic swell slumbered restlessly in the pitchy darkness.

Shemerelda sat in her dressing room in front of the mirror.

Her dress of sheer black satin was unadorned by flower or jewel.

She slipped off the shoulder straps and let it fall to her waist.

Her breasts stood out firm and full.

In the early days of their marriage Leonard would tread softly behind her and very gently powder the tips of her plum-red nipples.

This night he poked his head round the door of her dressing room and said:

"Shemerelda, my dear, are you ready? Our guests are due to arrive any minute."

Shemerelda turned to him and smiled.

He smiled, too, and nodded his head.

She hooked up her shoulder straps and arm in arm they descended the staircase and prepared to meet their guests.

The party was just swell.

How they danced in the ballroom.

How they ate in the buffet lounge.

Breasts of peacock, thighs of quail, liver of ptarmigan and beady eyes of plover – such goodies.

And how they gossiped, too.

"You see the fight last night?"

"Nope."

"You didn't see the fight last night?"

"Nope."

"I seen the fight last night. It sure was good."

The cream of the cream of Rackham City society was right in form.

As midnight struck Shemerelda noticed a man.

She had not seen him before.

He was tall and he was handsome.

"Leonard, who is that man?" she said.

Leonard smiled and slowly tapped the side of his nose with his forefinger.

"That, my dear Shemerelda, is the incredibly beautiful H. H. Washbrook."

Shemerelda inclined her head to the right and the man smiled briefly and fingered the deep, cool cleft in his chin.

What an incredibly beautiful chin.

Shemerelda danced and danced.

She whirled and she twirled.

Her smile never wavered.

"Darling Shemerelda, how exquisite you look tonight," said Mr Van Strjden, the entrepreneur.

"Shemerelda, your beauty is almost saintly," said Mr Ikin, the composer.

"You look great, Shemerelda, just great," said Mr Stollmeyer, the noted attorney.

At three in the morning Shemerelda stepped out through the french windows of the ballroom.

The night was balmy.

High overhead in the darkness geese called aloofly.

The sweet scents of the sandalwood drifted over the terrace.

The moon purred smugly.

Shemerelda skipped lightly down the curving flight of shallow stone steps to the gardens.

She took off her shoes and tossed free her golden hair.

Couples walked arm in arm on the gravel paths.

Couples embraced on the wrought iron benches.

Couples coupled in the whinnying arbors.

But not a soul saw Shemerelda as bare-footed, arms outstretched to the restless Atlantic swell, she glided gracefully over the lawns to the lower gardens where the Tozer tree bloomed.

She stood beneath its boughs.

She looked up into the rustling ranks of the scarlet blooms.

She slipped off the shoulder straps of her dress and pressed her naked breasts into two of the lowermost flowers.

"Tozer tree, Tozer tree," she whispered. "Where is love?"

A sharp cough.

She spun around.

A man stood behind her.

She clasped her hands to her breasts.

He was a stocky man.

His shoulders were broad and his hair was curly and grizzled.

On the bridge of his nose was a jagged white scar.

A cigar was clamped in the sickle of his mouth.

"You like the Tozer tree?" said the man.

Shemerelda nodded.

"I adore it," she said.

The man nodded.

He took the cigar from his mouth and tossed it to the ground.

He looked Shemerelda straight in the eyes, and then he stepped forward towards her.

She did not move.

Very gently he took her hands from her naked breasts.

Very gently with gnarled, strong hands he pulled up her dress and replaced it on her shoulders.

"What is your name?" he said.

"Shemerelda."

"Ah," he said. "Shemerelda."

And then he bowed stiffly.

"My name is Mirakel," he said. "We shall see much more of each other."

And then he was gone.

And the blooms of the Tozer tree whispered and chattered in the sudden breeze that sprang up from the nervous ocean.

chapter four

Who is the incredibly beautiful H. H. Washbrook?

Who is Mirakel?

Does love bloom in the springtime and die in the fall?

What panic grips the juices of the Tozer tree in the ice-chapped depths of winter?

That night Shemerelda slept not a wink.

chapter five

Three weeks later Shemerelda met Laverne Van Strjden at the South Rackhamshire Croquet and Real Tennis Club.

They had luncheon there.

"Shemerelda, honey, you look really really beautiful. Really," said Laverne Van Strjden.

Shemerelda flickered a smile.

She nodded.

"And so do you, Laverne," she said with scarcely a movement to her eyes.

"Nah, not me," said Laverne Van Strjden. "You know my trouble?"

Shemerelda shook her head softly.

"No, Laverne, I do not know your trouble," she said.

"I'm too loud," said Laverne Van Strjden, dolloping creamy puffs of powder to her eagline nose. "I gotta loud body – it screams at you. I gotta loud appearance – my wardrobe shrieks at you in agony. I gotta loud voice. If my voice were in a zoo, Shemerelda, you'd hope like hell it'd never breed."

Shemerelda took a sip of her hock and looked around her.

Mrs Estensen, the luncheon secretary, passed from table to table, rubbing her doe-soft hands beneath her chin and bowing as sly as a mousse.

The sailboats far out in the bay beyond the jetties smacked at the sun.

Mallets clacked and squabbled.

Waiters hovered, pointed as hawks.

"Shemerelda, honey, what you need is an affair," said Laverne Van Strjden, gulping loudly at her scotch. "I mean it. You never had one. Right? Sure I'm right. Well, listen to me, honey. The best thing I ever did in life was have my first affair."

She exhaled cigarette smoke.

Loudly.

"You wanta hear about it? Sure you do. It was Mr Van Strjden's head groom. An Argentinian. My dear, so handsome. And so rough. My God, it was like wrestling with a sackful of anacondas. And you should have heard him scream when he . . ."

Shemerelda held a golden droplet of hock in a moist, cool hollow of her tongue.

Her thoughts strayed to lands beyond the broad Atlantic.

She thought of gnarled castles on plunging cliffs.

She thought of half-timbered villages, hunched and huddled in a German mist.

She thought of paddle steamers churning a sullen river and of elvers wriggling in a trap of rushes.

". . . and then I had Mr Van Strjden's veterinarian. He was just out of college and, honey, I can't tell you how innocent. He knew all about canine hemorrhoids, but he sure as hell knew nothing about . . . well, let me tell you, my dear. The first time I got him into bed. Right? He was still wearing his left sock, and you'll never believe it, but I had to . . ."

They walked arm in arm from the dining room and established themselves in the lounge, where they took coffee.

". . . played the most sensational horn. Everything about him glistened. Know what I mean? Sure you do. You know, when he stepped out of the tub after we'd screwed, he still had this glistening . . ."

Shemerelda rolled the coffee round the roof of her mouth.

Dark tang of fig. Smoulder of rich, brooding cream.

She thought of red street cars clanking through narrow, cobbled streets.

She thought of fat-fingered priests and gypsy violinists with golden teeth.

She thought of the Danube sleeked by rain and of lambs' tongues spitting on wooden skewers.

". . . and, of course, he knew, honey. Mr Van Strjden knew of every single one. And he approved. Sure he did. He approved, because it saved him the bother himself. Right? Sure I'm right."

Her stockings rasped.

Loudly.

She placed her hand on Shemerelda's thigh.

"Shemerelda, honey, you need an affair. For Leonard's sake."

And then Shemerelda saw him once more.

He stepped from the locker room at the side of the real tennis courts.

He wore white kid jodphurs and a midnight blue silk short-sleeved shirt.

Around his neck was draped a loose ochre flannel towel.

Under his arm he carried three rackets.

"Laverne," said Shemerelda softly. "Do you know that man?"

Laverne Van Strjden arched her eyebrows over the top of her glass of scotch.

"Sure, honey. Sure I do," she said. "That is the incredibly beautiful H. H. Washbrook."

Freeway Eight strutted across Broken Arrow Meadows on slimsy concrete stilts.

In the winter the meadows were sodden with duck.

Now in the springtime the lazy creeks glistened and lisps of new-born flowers tipped the tongues of land that protruded into the flat-calm sea.

Shemerelda pressed firmly on the accelerator of her Umbertini-Jaguar.

The engine snarled proudly.

She felt its power deep in her loins.

To her right the skyscrapers of Rackham City gnawed the fringes of the stinging blue sky.

Ahead of her she saw the distant smudge of hills wherein nestled the gentle woods and tumbling streams of her childhood summers.

What summers!

Ancient charcoal burners tilting moleskin caps.

The romp and frisk of wild-flanked ponies.

Plump pies.

Possums.

Shemerelda smiled to herself and the Umbertini-Jaguar changed down a gear smugly as Freeway Eight curved down to the Eastport Interchange.

Ten minutes earlier she had left Laverne Van Strjden outside the beautician's parlor at the South Rackhamshire Croquet and Real Tennis Club.

"It won't do me no good, honey. But it might make the croquet mallets jealous," she had said and kissed Shemerelda on the cheek.

Loudly.

Right hand resting lightly on the steering wheel, Shemerelda guided the Umbertini-Jaguar through the bends and tender loops of the Interchange.

She had been on the Old Smugglers' Highway for not more than five minutes when she noticed the black limousine closing up rapidly behind her.

Curious.

It had been behind her all the way on Freeway Eight.

She remembered the sun flashing on the statuette on its hood.

She remembered clearly now its fastidiousness in keeping a constant distance behind her.

Now as the engine of the Umbertini-Jaguar drummed between the high wooded banks which lined the Highway the black limousine drew alongside her.

First she saw the statuette on the hood.

It was silver.

It was a condor's head.

Next she saw the face of the driver, staring impassively ahead.

He had a swarthy, olive skin and his cheekbones were high.

Next she saw the rear side windows of the limousine.

They were smoked black, and she could not see inside.

But acutely, achingly she was aware she was being watched.

The limousine kept its station alongside her.

She gripped the steering wheel tightly and reduced her speed as the Highway bent to the right.

The limousine did not flinch.

Its jet black flanks were no more than six inches from her side.

She was being watched.

Steadfastly.

Challengingly.

Menacingly.

Fear splintered against her nerve ends.

Panic frosted her blood.
She increased her speed.
Impassively the black limousine kept alongside her.
She reduced her speed.
Unerringly the black limousine followed suit.
And then nearer and nearer it began to edge towards her.
She could not change her course, for the ditch at the side of the Highway was deep, and its rutted edges were festered with the rotting leaves of the fall.
If she braked, wheels would spin and lock, her spine would snatch at its roots and snap, her heart would . . .
She braked.
Hard.
Even before her foot had hit the pedal the driver of the black limousine had sensed her move.
In an instant and a puff of blue smoke from his tyres, he reared away from her sinuously, and even before her car had commenced its shriek and its spin, he had disappeared from the Highway.
And a coven of small birds chattered in alarm.
Loudly.

The seat-belt kept Shemerelda secure and safe.
Luck and breeding kept the car on the road.
Breeding and beauty kept her ice-calm and serene as she docked the Umbertini-Jaguar on the gravel driveway in front of the vine-encrusted mansion and gave the keys to Blyton, the groom.
Ransome, the butler, met her in the hallway.
"Mr Tozer's compliments, madam," he said. "He wishes to inform you that he is dining with a client tonight and would be most grateful if you would dine alone in your rooms."
"Certainly, Ransome," said Shemerelda.
She took a long, slow bath.
She dined on poached Missouri brill and fillet of artichoke.
She read a slim volume of poems by Hannes Verlorener.
She browsed through her album of Cuban overfranks.
She stared at her naked breasts in the Louis Quinze hand mirror, and after a while she smiled.
At half past ten she left her rooms and descended the main staircase.

The hem of her Bruges lace skirt simpered behind her on the Afghan carpet and the lights of the Bohemian crystal chandeliers glowed lustrously in her massed blonde hair.

She was met at the foot of the staircase by her husband and his guest.

She recognised him at once.

"Mrs Tozer," he said with a sharp, downward plunge of his head.

He took her right hand and pressed it to his lips.

Very clearly she saw the jagged white scar on the bridge of his nose and the tight curls and grizzle of his hair.

"So pleased to meet you, Mrs Tozer."

Leonard took him by the arm.

"My dear Mirakel," he said. "You must call my wife Shemerelda. I'm sure you will be seeing much of her in the future."

Mirakel looked Shemerelda straight in the eyes.

"I'm sure I shall," he said. "Of that I am certain."

And with that Ransome, the butler, introduced the incredibly beautiful H. H. Washbrook to their presence.

chapter six

And so Shemerelda took a lover.

Oh, the passion.

Oh, the heaving of limbs and the soft sighs of requited joy.

Oh, the ecstasy.

Oh, the gush and pump of juices, the slide and glide of flesh, the . . .

But not so fast.

No need to hurry.

After all, painted birds still sing on the laden boughs of the Tozer tree.

chapter seven

At breakfast next morning Leonard, rich and plump and young as well, said:

"I hope you slept well last night, Shemerelda."

Shemerelda said:

"Yes, I did, thank you, Leonard. I hope you, too, slept well."

Leonard smiled at her.

"Thank you, my dear," he said. "I did."

But he lied.

All night long he had tossed and turned in his lonesome bed.

The sough of the wind in the eaves of the roof had mocked his sleeplessness.

The roll and rumble of the Atlantic breakers had taunted the fruitless surges of his passions.

At three in the morning he rose from his bed.

He put on his robe and left his bedroom.

He padded softly along the corridor on damp-soled feet.

Cautiously he opened the door of Shemerelda's bedroom.

Breathlessly he stepped inside.

Shemerelda lay naked on top of the coverlet.

Moonlight cast cool, deep shadows in her thighs.

The scented night breezelet whispered the tips of her golden hair across her firm and full young breasts.

A pulse in her neck fluttered.

Leonard advanced towards the bed.

He looked down on Shemerelda.

Slowly she parted her thighs, and for an instant the rift between her loins with the nestling's gape flirted with the moonlight.

"Shemerelda, Shemerelda," said Leonard very quietly.

Very quietly indeed.

That was all.

'Only three lines'

He returned to his bedroom.
And languorously Shemerelda opened her eyes and smiled.
It was a contented smile.

chapter eight

"I am to travel to Venezuela on business, Shemerelda," said Leonard. "I shall be away for at least one week."

"Ah," said Shemerelda.

They were taking tea on the lower lawn.

The Tozer tree bloomed louringly.

A fiery orange oriole piped creamily.

A chimney swift twisted and chippered.

"I propose to take you for luncheon tomorrow. I hope the plan is agreeable to you," said Leonard.

"It is," said Shemerelda.

"After that I shall buy you a gift."

"Ah," said Shemerelda.

Leonard's office suite occupied the whole of the thirty-ninth floor of the Tozer Building on Sixth Avenue in downtown Rackham City.

Shemerelda waited for her husband in the reception lounge.

She looked out of the window.

The view was superb.

Beneath her Rackham Island nosed into the broad, sun-dappled waters of the Downey River.

Wharves and warehouses huddled its shores.

Brownstone houses peeked above gentle leafy squares.

A snow-white ocean liner ruffled the river's blue as tug boats huffed it to the jetty.

"A stunning view, Mrs Tozer."

Shemerelda turned.

Facing her was her husband's secretary, Rogan Shieff.

He was young.

He was handsome.

And he was slim.

His suit was cut with elegance.

His tan was firm and easy.

And his teeth were white and even.

She smiled.

"I do hope Mr Tozer's absence on business does not incommode you too greatly," said Rogan Shieff.

"Ah," said Shemerelda.

"On this occasion I shall not be accompanying him," said Rogan Shieff, offering Shemerelda a cigarette from a slim Cadiz-gold case.

She shook her head.

"If I can be of service to you at any time, please do not hesitate to contact me," said Rogan Shieff.

And he lowered his eyelids and pursed his lips.

Leonard and Shemerelda took luncheon at Massimo's on East Forty-Ninth.

Leonard chose fettucini, roast hazel hen with chestnut and salami stuffing, and Modena burlice tart with Tuscan clotted cream.

Shemerelda chose asparagus tips in aspic.

"What will you do whilst I am away on business, Shemerelda?" said Leonard as he sipped his Strega and puffed at his Dom Rosa cigar.

"This and that, Leonard," said Shemerelda. "This and that."

Leonard signed for his check with a pen of Aztec silver and escorted Shemerelda to the restaurant exit.

The bullet-silver Bentley-Strossner was waiting for them.

"To Henshley's department store, if you please, Milne," said Leonard to the chauffeur.

He held Shemerelda's wrist as the automobile purred through the lazy traffic.

"I intend to buy you something that will remind you of me while I am gone, Shemerelda," he said.

"How nice, Leonard," said Shemerelda.

"I intend to buy you a pet."

"Thank you."

Leonard and Shemerelda were greeted at the main entrance to Henshley's Department store by Mr Kruger Henshley the Third.

He took them to his office and gave them sherry in glasses of Galway crystal.

Then he ushered them to the third floor and introduced them to the curator of pets, Mr Baines Reed.

"I leave you in his most capable hands, Mr Tozer," he said, and he bowed to Shemerelda and let his eyes rest briefly on her slim and shapely ankles.

"You may choose anything you will, Shemerelda," said Leonard. "All I ask is that it is something that will be a remembrance of me."

Shemerelda looked around.

Dogs yapped and bayed and greeted them with the red carpets of their tongues.

Fila Brasileiros from Brazil, Owtcharkas from Russia, Zwergpinschers from Germany, Xoloitcuintlis from Mexico, Springers from Wales, Alanos from Spain – what a whinnying of tails and a thumping of canine hearts.

A black panther cub brooded.

A kinkajou sulked.

An otter dozed steamily.

"Look around you, Shemerelda. Take your time," said Leonard.

Ranks of monkeys.

Macaques from Japan, geladas from Ethiopia, capuchins, tamarins, lorises, mangabeys and pottos from Africa – what a yattering, a yakkering, a yanking of bars.

"Choose what you wish, Shemerelda," said Leonard.

Cages of birds.

Combassous, lorikeets, black-billed mynahs, cordon bleus, tanagers, pittas, buff-bellied hummingbirds, ruby-crowned kinglets – my, what a flickering, a snickering, a tickering of avian hearts.

"Make your choice, Shemerelda," said Leonard. "Only let it be a memento of me."

"Of course," said Shemerelda.

She chose a skink.

Its neck was thick.

Its legs were short.

Its scales were slimy and its eyes were opaque.

"And, Leonard," said Shemerelda.

"Yes, Shemerelda?" said Leonard.

"I should like you to buy a black velvet choker mounted with rubies to put around its neck."

Leonard nodded.

"Certainly, Shemerelda," he said. "But of course."

chapter nine

And so the jet plane, Venezuela-bound, scythes into the rolling prairies of the sky.

The skink skulks in its cage.

Strings of barges hump upstream into the Downey River.

Locomotives whine at the night.

Salmon spawn in tumbling mountain streams.

Charcoal burners slumber draughtily.

A signet ring inscribed with a condor's head flashes briefly in the shadow of a bartender's smile.

And what of Shemerelda?

What of her love?

Indeed, who is he?

Wait.

Be patient.

chapter ten

On the evening after Leonard's departure for Venezuela Laverne Van Strjden invited Shemerelda to dinner.

She arrived at six thirty.

Her gown crooned to the contours of her body.

A fleck of spittle appeared on Mr Van Strjden's lower lip.

He took her into the music room and offered her cocktails.

"Thank you," said Shemerelda.

Mr Van Strjden, minute and middle-aged and rich as well, licked his upper lip with a carp-like tongue.

"Laverne will be down presently," he said.

"Good," said Shemerelda.

Mr Van Strjden squinted his eyes.

"My dear Shemerelda, you look extremely beautiful tonight," he said.

"Thank you."

"Such beauty in a woman has its dangers, my dear."

"Ah."

"The straight and narrow path of virtue is strewn with mines, and in every thicket there lurks a predator."

"Ahah."

A hyacinth macaw on a Sheffield steel stand rattled its food bowl with a scowled beak.

Mr Van Strjden took Shemerelda by the arm and led her to a chaise-longue of Uppsala brocade.

He sat down beside her and placed his hand lightly on her thigh.

She smiled.

"I would not wish Laverne to know what I am about to tell you," he said.

"Naturally," said Shemerelda.

Mr Van Strjden coughed and the pressure of his hand upon her thigh increased.

"Shortly after our marriage I became enamored of a much younger woman than myself."

"Ah," said Shemerelda.

"She was an extremely beautiful woman.

"We established a relationship.

"A clandestine relationship.

"Neither her husband nor my wife was aware of our liaison."

He paused and placed his other hand upon Shemerelda's shoulder.

"I wonder, Shemerelda, if you are aware of the gist of my little talk with you," he said.

Shemerelda smiled.

"Perfectly aware, Mr Van Strjden," she said.

"Good," said Mr Van Strjden. "I am delighted that we now know where we stand."

Laverne Van Strjden came down from her dressing room in a volley of perfume and a broadside of rouge.

"My God, don't I look revolting?" she said, and she took her husband in her arms and embraced him.

Loudly.

Mr Van Strjden excused himself and repaired to his study.

Laverne Van Strjden looked down on Shemerelda as she reclined on the chaise-longue and said:

"Shemerelda, honey, you look divine."

"Thank you, Laverne," said Shemerelda.

"I mean it. I really do. What a bosom. And no brassiere. My God, I can see your nipples. I really can. Nipples. That's what drives men crazy. You know my gangster lover? You don't. I'll tell you. He used to look at me and he'd say: 'Sweetheart, you got the greatest pair of tits in the whole of Rackham City, but you ain't got no nipples.' He was right. I ain't. I got ingrowing nipples. You know? My Argentinian used to put his mouth round them, and he'd . . ."

The walls of the music room were lined with old music frames in Sudanese yucca wood.

Bruckner, Mahler, Chopin, Brahms, Zuccioni – what names!

There was a virginal from Madrid, a zither from the Tirol, a vina from India – what novel instruments.

There was a set of bagpipes from Scotland – what a disgusting contraption.

". . . so on account of my Persian gentleman I got hooked on waxing my legs. You have to wax your legs, Shemerelda? Sure you don't. My God, the pain. Why am I so hairy, Shemerelda? Course there are men who like hairy women. It drives them crazy. Did I ever tell you about my tennis coach and the time he and I . . ."

The floor of the music room was inlaid with Dutch delft tiles.

The ceiling was baroque with naked nymphs couched on rumbling white clouds.

Logs burned in the fireplace of green Capozzi marble.

A flat-eyed Simba cat slumbered on the numdah rug.

". . . yet you, Shemerelda, hell, you always look so cool. You know what I mean? Sure you do. Cool. Cool, Shemerelda."

Laverne Van Strjden inhaled loudly on her Lucky Strike cigarette and grinned.

"Well, honey," she said. "You won't be so cool, when I tell you who your dinner partner is."

"Really, Laverne?" said Shemerelda. "And who is my partner to be?"

Laverne paused and then said in a loud voice:

"The incredibly beautiful H. H. Washbrook."

Shemerelda's heart missed a cool beat.

How the incredibly beautiful H. H. Washbrook talked over dinner.

He told of his travels.

He told of slow, yearning sunsets on the Perfume River.

He told of thin-lipped dhows flimsing the waters of Araby.

He told of ice flows gnashing the Dnieper River, of the throat-parched deserts of Africay, of jungles screaming with the pain of small-furred animals.

"Gee," said Laverne Van Strjden. "Gee. What d'ya know?"

The incredibly beautiful H. H. Washbrook told of his adventures.

He told of gun fights in Marseilles, of fist fights in Singapore.

He told of the stampede of buffalo, the charge of rhino, the red-rimmed howl of the wounded boar at bay.

"Most interesting, Mr Washbrook. Most interesting," said Mr Van Strjden, and dapperly he snapped off a piece of popadom, and dapperly he smiled at Shemerelda.

The incredibly beautiful H. H. Washbrook told of his experiences in urbania.

He told of the gilded rooftops of Istanbul, the minarets of Qum, the cobbled marts of London town, the Jen Min Lu of old Shanghai.

Shemerelda was entranced.

Shemerelda was enchanted.

Such an incredibly beautiful man.

Such incredibly beautiful stories.

And the way he looked at her.

No wonder her nipples swelled and hardened.

No wonder her loins ached and yearned.

At the end of the evening the incredibly beautiful H. H. Washbrook placed his bronzed and manly arm upon her shoulder and asked her softly so no one would hear if he might drive her home.

Shemerelda looked at him with love in her eyes and lust in her heart.

"We shall see," she said. "We shall see."

chapter eleven

So who is he?
Who is the guy?
For heaven's sake, who is Shemerelda's lover?
Mirakel of the grizzled hair?
Mr Van Strjden, minute and middle-aged and rich as well?
The incredibly beautiful H. H. Washbrook?
All three?
How calm she is.
How serene.
How beautiful.
Only the finest and choicest of lover is good enough for her.
Please, Shemerelda, please, do not lightly cede your charms.

chapter twelve

On the third day of Leonard's business sojourn in Venezuela Shemerelda received a phone call.

It was from Mirakel.

"Shemerelda?"

"Yes."

"This is Mirakel."

"I know."

It was ten o'clock of the morning.

Shemerelda lay in her bed.

Her long lissom legs were entwined around the coverlet of purest Shantung silk.

Her long blonde hair lay atumble on the pillows of softest percale.

Her firm full breasts soared through her nightdress of finest Oxford voile.

"Shemerelda, I have something to ask you."

"Yes?"

"Will you become my lover?"

"Yes."

Crash of breaker on Atlantic strand.

Shriek of seabird above spitting surf.

Heave and gush of elemental fire in jungles of primeval darkness.

"I know of a place where we can meet."

"Good."

"I will give you the address, and you will meet me within the hour."

"Good."

Mirakel gave Shemerelda the address.

He hung up.

Shemerelda dressed.

She went downstairs.

She opened the front door.

She went outside.
She entered the Umbertini-Jaguar.
She started the Umbertini-Jaguar.
She drove down the gravel driveway and turned into the Old Smugglers' Highway bound for the city and her assignation.
The wind whipped back her chiffon scarf.
The Umbertini-Jaguar preened back the Highway.
The trees waved their boughs, and the rich green grasses and sedges sighed and seered.
Shemerelda smiled and sang softly to herself.
Oh, bliss.
Oh, happiness.
What Shemerelda did not see was the black limousine with the condor's head statuette that closed in behind her as she sidled into the Eastport Interchange and kept behind her as she drove deep into the heart of Rackham City.

Westside Rackham City – what a racial melting pot.
A positive ethnic casserole.
A veritable phyletic fricasee.
Shemerelda drove slowly through the narrow, twisting streets, looking for the address Mirakel had given her.
On the sidewalks an animated phylogentic frieze.
Mongoloid folds, needling Semite teeth, hawkish Kamite nose, swagger of Teuton, sway and shuffle of swarthy Ethiop.
The bustle, the clamor, the noise, the shivaree.
The smells.
Shemerelda felt her heartbeats quicken.
Her skin tingled, her eyes sparkled, the secret voices locked fast inside the dark vaults of memory broke free and sang and soared.
Alcott Street!
The very place.
Shemerelda turned right and entered a canyon of sullen, red-brick apartment blocks, pinched and narrow-chested, dull-eyed and cowed.
She scanned the house numbers eagerly.
Hard slap on brakes.
Dog yap and scuttle.
Number nineteen.

Farther to go.
Past oozing laundry.
Past drunk-fested steps. Past paddy-whacked bar. Past oaf and liar. Past runt and cripple.
Number Eighty One.
That's it.
The Mount Stowe Hotel.
Shemerelda pulled the Umbertini-Jaguar alongside the sidewalk.
She locked the door of the automobile behind her.
Without looking to right or left she crossed the hump-backed sidewalk and entered the hotel.
What she did not see was the black limousine with the condor's head statuette draw to a halt ten yards behind the Umbertini-Jaguar.
Neither did she see the smoked-black rear windows wind down and the glint of a pair of incredibly beautiful eyes.

Shemerelda entered the lobby of the Mount Stowe Hotel.
A stout bald man in aged sweat-shirt sat behind the desk, picking his teeth with a pin.
He did not look up.
"I wonder if you could direct me to the room of . . ."
"Sure, lady, sure. Room Eighteen. The elevator don't work. You gotta use the stairs."
Pitter pat of heart as Shemerelda ascended the stairs.
Peeling walls, scabrous handrail, sloughing snake of carpet.
She knocked on the door of Room Eighteen.
It was opened immediately.
"Shemerelda!"
"Mirakel!"
He stood there naked to the waist.
He took her left hand and kissed it.
"Shemerelda," he said. "Come inside and let us make love."

chapter thirteen

How to describe that scene of carnal ardor?

A bedroom simple and austere.

A table.

A chair.

A bed.

On the bed lies Shemerelda.

Her spoondrift of golden hair eddies and swells over full firm breasts.

Her golden thicket shimmers.

She parts her lips.

She parts her thighs.

Mirakel stands beside her.

His flag is proud and erect.

He straddles her.

His tongue explores the rims of nipples, taut and tense.

His tongue explores the sighing shadows beneath her breasts.

His tongue rides the swell of her belly.

Slowly he shifts his position and turns.

Her mouth reaches out to his loins.

Her tongue begins to . . .

But no.

Let us not intrude.

Let us leave them to their reverie.

Let us return, when desire is sated, and the cataracts of passion lie slack, and love is the sweet mist that softly hangs above the still evening lake of memory.

Wow!

chapter fourteen

"Mirakel. Oh, Mirakel."

Shemerelda lay in her lover's arms.

Dusk sloped in through the windows and calmed the contours of the chair and lapped the flimsy curtain's hem.

"It was so good, Mirakel. It was so right and so proper."

Shemerelda ran her fingers through her lover's hair.

She kissed his mouth.

"When I was a little girl, my father employed two woodmen.

"One was in his prime.

"He had broad shoulders and his waist was slim. The hairs on his chest were tangled and his forearms rippled in the sun.

"He was just like you.

"The other was a youth.

"He was shy and he blushed a lot.

"His skin was so delicate. His hands were so shy. His smile made me weep with joy.

"He, too, was just like you."

Shemerelda wrapped her thighs around her lover's waist.

She ran her hands over the nape of his neck.

"Our house was always full of laughter.

"We had big dogs.

"In the paddocks my father kept Appaloosas and Morgans and Connemara ponies.

"There was a lake where my brothers fished.

"My grandfather had a cork leg.

"The land was never still when it snowed, and there was a hawk owl that jerked its tail, and my grandfather would talk of the days when he hunted fox in the Hudson Bay.

"My mother had a maid called Rosa.

"She came from Riga."

Shemerelda placed her tongue inside her lover's ear.

It grew dark.

"My father's brother never married.

"He lived with us.

"He went to the wars and when he returned, he used to sit on the porch and smile."

A squabble of children on the sidewalk outside. Siren yowl. Gurgle and splat of cough.

"My hair was always very long.

"My sister's hair was long, too.

"Once she got a turtle as a present.

"The janitor built a pond for it.

"It died because she forgot to feed it."

Shemerelda drew away from her lover.

She propped herself on her elbows and looked down on him.

"And now, Mirakel," she said. "Tell me something about yourself."

He looked up at her.

"No, Shemerelda," he said. "Go home."

chapter fifteen

Not a word did Shemerelda hear from Mirakel.

Rain coiled in from the Atlantic and soaked the blossoms of the Tozer tree.

Petals lay sodden on the lawn.

Leonard telephoned from Maracaibo.

The weather was clement, although the humidity was causing him some bronchial discomfort.

The food was moderately palatable.

His accommodation was tolerable.

He had had to buy three pairs of socks.

"I miss you, Shemerelda," he said.

"Do you, Leonard?"

"Yes."

And Shemerelda replaced the receiver.

For three whole days she hovered around the phone.

Laverne Van Strjden rang.

Would she care to meet her for luncheon at the South Rackhamshire Croquet and Real Tennis Club?

No.

How about luncheon at the Eastport Yacht Club?

No.

Mrs Passau rang to invite her for an evening of bridge at her residence at Beecher's Quay.

She declined.

Admiral and Mrs Kolokof wondered if she would care to attend an intimate party to celebrate the engagement of their elder daughter, Clovissa, to Mr Edwin Culpepper, the noted toxicologist.

She would not.

On the morning of the fourth day Rogan Shieff rang.

"I wonder if we could meet, Mrs Tozer," he said.

Shemerelda said nothing.

"It is most urgent. It concerns your husband."

"I see."

Where was Mirakel?

Why had he not rung?

Was he ill?

Was he dead?

"Mrs Tozer?"

"Yes?"

"Ah, I was wondering if you were still there."

"Yes I am."

"Perhaps then we could meet later this morning."

"Yes. If you arrive here at twelve o'clock, I shall be prepared to meet you."

A pause.

Mirakel, Mirakel, Mirakel – her heart pumped in time to the rhythms of his name.

Did he hate her?

Did he despise her?

Did he think nothing of her?

Had she been a mere plaything?

A diversion?

A quick lay to be sung about in smoke-filled taverns or snickering locker rooms?

Another notch in the crutch of his self-esteem?

"I would rather we meet some place else, Mrs Tozer."

Another pause.

Whiskers of rain scratched at the windows of her dressing room.

"You see, Mrs Tozer, the matters I have to discuss are of an extremely delicate nature.

"Discretion is imperative.

"As a matter of fact, Mrs Tozer, I have taken the liberty of booking for two at the Smugglers' Inn on Beecher's Quay for luncheon today.

"I suggest we meet at twelve forty-five."

Mirakel, Mirakel, Mirakel – she remembered the cry he gave at the moment of her first climax.

A cry of ecstasy?

Or a cry of triumph?

The cry of the lover?

Or the cry of the conqueror?

"Well then, Mrs Tozer, that's settled.

"Smugglers' Inn. Twelve forty-five.

"I look forward to meeting you."

He rang off.

Mirakel.

Oh, Mirakel, where are you?

Beecher's Quay lay at the tip of a spit of land.

The spit of land arched its way into the Downey River at the point where it flopped itself into the bold Atlantic.

The estuary was broad and hazy with distance.

In the fall and in the early springtime it was a piping, fluttering confetti of wader birds.

In the winter it thundered with ice-bellied storms or stood sentinel, clear and simple, and aching with cold.

Now it lay, restless and uneasy, furrowed with squalls of rain and lumbered with low, gray clouds.

The harbor at Beecher's Quay was long since silted up.

The fine clapboard houses creaked.

In the summer they lowered their shutters and hid their gaze from the summer frolickers, the brittle playthings of the sun, the charcoal burners of steaks – frying pantheists to a man.

Shemerelda remembered her grandfather's stories of distant smudgy days when immigrants crept ashore in creaking mists, and coastguard cutters snuffled and bootleggers scuffled and snarled.

And long long before those days the proud clippers had set sail for the ports of Europe – the sullen harbors of the Baltic, the sulky havens of the Mediterranean, the booze-bound havens of foggy Albion.

It was twelve forty-three.

Shemerelda parked the Umbertini-Jaguar at the rear of the Smugglers' Inn.

She pulled up the collar of her white Burberry and stepped out into the rain.

She smelled salt-tang and seaweed-snarl.

She saw a steamer racked with black smoke churning against the tide.

She saw a knot of dowitcher probing nervously on the shore.

At twelve forty-five precisely she entered the front door of the Smugglers' Inn.

Rogan Shieff was waiting for her.

He wore a cream linen suit.

His shirt was apple-green with white polka dots. His shoes were strawberry brogue. In his lapel he wore a navy blue carnation.

"Mrs Tozer," he said as he led her to a table in a bottle-green bow fronted window. "I have taken the liberty of ordering you a small dry sherry."

"I prefer lime juice, if you please," said Shemerelda.

Rogan Shieff raised his eyebrows a fraction.

"But, of course," he said and he summoned the waiter with a flick of his fingers and ordered the drink Shemerelda desired.

He sat down opposite her and rested his hands on the table.

Hands with a free and easy tan.

Hands with fingernails half-mooned and honed.

"Mrs Tozer," he said after a moment. "Or may I call you Shemerelda?"

"Mrs Tozer."

He smiled.

Flash of white even teeth.

The merest curl of upper lip. The briefest narrowing of eyes.

"As you wish," he said.

Shemerelda took a sip of her lime juice.

His anthracite-black eyes followed her every move.

She did not flinch from his gaze.

"Mrs Tozer, have you ever wondered why for the first time in my association with your husband I have not accompanied him on a business trip?"

"No."

"Does it occur to you that he might have substantial reasons for my not being with him in Venezuela?"

"No."

Mirakel.

Mirakel of the pumping buttocks.

Mirakel of the juicy, probing tongue.

Mirakel of the upward surge and thrust of hips.

"I find that most curious, Mrs Tozer."

"Do you indeed?"

"Yes I do."

He leaned back and draped his right arm over the back of his chair.

His movements were elegant, self-assured.

Well-rehearsed, too.

"Mrs Tozer, I have information about your husband's activities, which might well prove detrimental to him."

"I see."

"And, of course, ultimately, Shemerelda, to you yourself."

He smiled once more.

"You are a very beautiful woman, Mrs Tozer. I am sure you are desired by very many men."

Mirakel.

Mirakel of the sinewed thighs.

Mirakel of the whipcord neck.

Mirakel of the bullet-scarred chest.

"I think I do not flatter myself when I say I am not without attractions to the opposite sex."

"You do not."

He inched his fingers slowly across the table towards her hand, which lightly held the glass of lime juice.

"Shemerelda, I have the feeling – the strong feeling – that we might be able to reach an accommodation on this matter."

She opened her mouth and ran her tongue lightly over her moist lower lip.

"There is no reason why the harmful information I have regarding your husband should ever be revealed."

"Is there not?"

"We are adult folk, you and I, Shemerelda. We are both desirable people. We have a lot to offer each other. You follow my meaning?"

"Yes."

He placed his hand on her hand.

He placed his thumb against her palm.

Very slowly he rubbed it up and down.

"My apartment is most discreet. Let us go there now, Shemerelda. Let us go there and discuss my proposition in more propitious circumstances. What do you say, Shemerelda? What do you say?"

She looked him straight in the eyes.

She smiled.

And then she hurled her glass of lime juice in his face.

She left at once.

chapter sixteen

"Mirakel, I love you.
"I love you, Mirakel. I adore you."
A bedroom simple and austere.
A table.
A chair.
A bed.
Shemerelda snuggled close to her lover.
He shifted slightly in the bed and placed his arm around her shoulder.
She rested her head on his chest and nuzzled at his nipples.
She took his free hand and placed it on her golden thicket.
Two hours earlier she had returned from her assignation at the Smugglers' Inn.
No sooner had she slipped out of her white Burberry than the phone rang.
"Shemerelda!"
"Mirakel!"
"You will meet me?"
"Yes. When?"
"Today. Same place as before. In an hour. You can make that?"
"Of course."
She summoned Milne, the chauffeur.
She established herself in the deep slumbering rear seat of the Bentley-Strossner and closed her eyes to the sleeking rain and the stuttering wind as the automobile purred into the centre of the city.
She disembarked at Byrne Street elevated railway station.
"Here, madame? Here?" said Milne, the chauffeur, as he opened the rear door of the Bentley-Strossner.
"Here, Milne," said Shemerelda. "You may return home immediately."

Milne, the chauffeur, had watched her bound up the clangful steps to the station.

A fang of a smile had come to his lips.

Rattle and lurch of the El.

Canal and wharf.

Backside of tenement. Broken-backed automobiles squatting whore-like in deserted streets. Tallow factory wheezing.

The lobby of the Mount Stowe Hotel.

A mound of cardboard suitcases and a seaman's battered chest.

"Same room, lady. Number Eighteen. The elevator still don't work."

Pitter pat of heart.

Knock on door.

"Shemerelda!"

"Mirakel!"

Without speaking he had removed her clothes.

He had stepped back and looked at her silently for a while as she stood naked and motionless in the centre of the room.

Gently he had led her to the bed.

Fiercely he had made love to her.

Fiercely, urgently, ravenously she had cried out with exaltation.

And now as fiercely, urgently, ravenously the rain beat at the windows she lay in her lover's arms and murmured and moaned as his calm tender fingers explored the cool glade at the centre of her thicket of gold.

She kissed his mouth.

"I was fifteen the first time I visited Rackham City.

"We went by train.

"My grandmother met us at the station and took us for luncheon at Henshley's department store.

"She bought me a pink velvet dress.

"She said to me: 'Shemerelda, you are growing a bosom.'"

She felt the quickened movement of Mirakel's probing fingers, and she arched her back and narrowed her eyes and ran her teeth over her lower lip.

"I was seventeen when I realised people thought I was beautiful.

"I was so slow.

"I did not suspect a thing.

"My elder brother's friend came home on furlough.

"We had a family picnic by the lake, and my brothers and my father were fishing.

"I remember it so well.

"My brother's friend ran his hand down the length of my hair.

"I started to tremble.

"He opened my shirt and placed his hand inside.

"He trembled, too.

"And when I looked into his eyes, I knew I was beautiful."

She looked into Mirakel's eyes.

She shivered.

Jet plane roar.

Bleat of locomotive.

Wail of ship siren.

"My grandfather died in the fall.

"We took him to the graveyard in the knock-kneed buggy, and old Ambrose, the Hafflinger, pulled it.

"We placed his cork leg in a separate coffin.

"It came on to snow, and that was the first time I saw Leonard."

Voices from next door bedroom.

A nasal whine. Guttural bark.

Snark of laughter.

"Everyone thought Leonard would marry my sister.

"But my sister died.

"She wasted away to nothing, and I sat by her bed all day long and throughout the night.

"Everyone wept at the funeral.

"Someone sent a spray of mimosa for her coffin.

"I slipped away on my own.

"I walked and I walked and I walked.

"I came to the glade where the charcoal burners had their hut. I went inside and it was lit by an old lamp. They said not a word to me. They drew up a chair and I sat down. I couldn't see them. They were in the shadows. But I knew they were watching me and I knew they were grieving for me. They ate their evening meal but they did not offer me food.

"They were quite silent.

"Leonard and his father found me.

"My father had sent out search parties.

"I spoke more to Leonard that night than I have ever spoken to him since."

She turned to her lover and bit his neck.

Hard.

She drew blood.

"Now, Mirakel," she said. "Tell me something about you."

He turned his head to her.

He smiled.

"No, Shemerelda," he said. "It is time for you to leave."

She dressed quickly.

Mirakel did not move from the bed.

She closed the door of room Eighteen softly behind her.

She hurried through the lobby.

As she stepped off the sidewalk and crossed the street she did not see the black limousine with the condor's head statuette nor the pair of incredibly beautiful eyes that watched her intently until she hailed the cab and stepped inside.

It was a knock-kneed cab.

chapter seventeen

Beware, Shemerelda.

Take care.

A dapper man smiles to himself as in his music room he dapperly polishes the drone on his Scottish bagpipes.

A man with a firm and easy tan seethes with rage.

He fumes.

A chauffeur gossips.

He smirks.

A plump man, rich and balding and young as well, sits in the drawing room of his hotel suite and opens a cablegram.

He reads it slowly.

Intently.

He smiles to himself.

It is a contented smile.

Take care, Shemerelda.

Beware.

chapter eighteen

Mr Van Strjden entertained his guests with the music of Handel and Vivaldi.

They were on a yacht.

It was Mr Van Strjden's yacht.

Dressed overall, the craft white and cool as an egret, curved softly away from the jetty of the South Rackhamshire Croquet and Real Tennis Club.

How the guests talked.

"You see the ball game last night?"

"Nope."

"You didn't see the ball game last night?"

"Nope."

"I seen the ball game last night. It sure was good."

The cream of the cream of Rackham City Society was right in form.

Shemerelda reclined on a deck-chair.

The music, constrained and urbane, ruffled through the awnings and trembled with the wind.

Gulls rode easy on stiff-shouldered currents of air.

The sun blazed.

"Telephone for you, Mrs Tozer."

Shemerelda opened her eyes.

The steward bowed and offered the telephone on a silver platter.

She picked up the receiver.

"Yes?"

"Shemerelda?"

"Yes."

"It's Leonard."

"Yes."

"I'm ringing to tell you that my return home will be somewhat delayed."

"I see."

"As soon as my schedules are finalised I shall contact you and give you precise details of my return."

"Thank you."

"The weather is good here today."

"I see."

"How is the weather with you?"

"Good."

The steward bowed once more and removed the telephone.

Shemerelda rose from the deck-chair.

She rested her arms on the rails of the yacht.

Gentle swell.

The swell of Mirakel.

Salty juices of the ocean.

The juices of Mirakel.

The yacht hugged the shore of Rackham Island.

Golden strands wasted away to bluffs of concrete and steel piers of the first of the bridges.

The skyscrapers of the city soared above the roosted cliffs of apartment blocks.

The river narrowed.

The tenements of the mainland teemed in.

A black man fishing on a rubbled shore. Children diving from a stump of iron. Flare and shriek of welder's gun.

The river gave way to the East Channel that sliced the island from the mainland.

Bucking, foaming shallows.

Tugboat and lighter.

Brace of rusting bridges.

Joggers in the park.

Heave and thrust of yacht.

The heave and thrust of Mirakel.

"Shemerelda, honey, you look just swell."

Laverne Van Strjden, loud as a forest in the fall, grasped Shemerelda round the waist and spun her to face her.

She held her at arms length. She nodded her head. She clicked her tongue.

And she chuckled.

"So it's true?" she said.

"What is true, Laverne?" said Shemerelda.

Laverne Van Strjden threw back her head and roared with laughter.

Loudly.

Then quite suddenly she stopped.

A flicker of inner fire passed briefly across her eyes.

Very softly she said:

"Shemerelda, you got yourself a lover."

Shemerelda brushed a strand of golden hair from her eyes.

"Oh, sweetheart, you're still as cool as ever. Still as distant. Right? But I can see. You gotta lover. Right? Sure I am."

Soar of fiddles.

Chutter of viols.

Triumphant cry of trumpet.

Nosing out of the East Channel, Mr Van Strjden's egretine yacht rimmed the northern shores of Rackham Island.

Piers for tramp and ocean liner.

Fireboats.

Stilted wings and snarling bank of seaplane.

Warehouse and old-crone church.

Ancient Dutch fort with drooping cannons.

Laverne Van Strjden sat next to Shemerelda in the Ladies' Saloon.

"Honey," she said softly once more. "I know who your lover is."

Shemerelda reclined her head to the right and raised her eyebrows.

"Mrs Kolokof saw you. Right? She saw you with your lover."

The yacht yawed slowly to port and a driblet of scotch splashed onto Laverne Van Strjden's lap.

"Shit," she said.

On the walls of the Saloon were paintings by Klimt and Khnopff, Toorop and Strahtmann and Pinky Marcius-Simmons.

There were drawings by Moreau and Beardsley and prints by Benois, Bakst and Korovine.

Laverne Van Strjden leaned her mouth towards Shemerelda's ear and whispered:

"The name of your lover, my dear Shemerelda, is Rogan Shieff."

She drew back and nodded her head rapidly.

"Right, Shemerelda? Am I right? Sure I am."

Shemerelda smiled softly.

Through the windows of the Ladies' Saloon she saw the golden pinnacles of the Tozer Building knifing at the evening sky.

"Sensational, honey. What a catch. Sensational."

Gently the yacht eased its way into the full flood tide of the Downey River.

Gently it heeled to port and gracefully dipped its bow and curtseyed.

And the sun hung its head and slipped away to the gentle smudge of the distant mainland hills.

"My God, I'm so envious, Shemerelda. Those eyes. Those teeth. And what a figure. Sensational. And how is he in bed, honey? Don't tell me. Sensational. Right? Sure I'm right."

Shemerelda smiled.

"That smile tells me everything, honey. You know what it is? It's beatific. It's like the smile on the face of them dames Mr Van Strjden's got stuck on the walls of this goddam saloon. You know that? Too damn right."

Laverne Van Strjden poured herself another large scotch.

Her fingernails flashed scarlet.

Her jewelled wrists jangled and splintered the soft filtering of early dusk.

"You gotta take my advice, Shemerelda. Be careful. You know what I mean? Sure you do. The situation is good. But it's tricky. Know what I mean? Don't let him use you. Know what I mean? Don't get involved in the work side. If he starts asking you favours from Leonard, wowee, give him the hardest kick in the balls he's ever had. Know what I mean? Sure you do. Listen, honey, I had a fling with Mr Van Strjden's personal bodyguard, and I can tell you – watch out. This guy was the biggest goddam leech I ever . . ."

Gentle purr and throb of yacht engines.

Sparkle and zest of Vivaldi.

Mirakel.

Mirakel, Mirakel, oh, Mirakel.

". . . and he takes me to see his momma. His momma, for chrissakes. We get the ferry to Selsey. We take a cab to this crummy wooden shack, and there's this crummy old dame sitting on the crummy porch smoking a pipe. A pipe, for chrissakes, honey. I turned to him and I said . . ."

Shemerelda stood up.

She walked to the door of the Ladies' Saloon.

"See you later, Laverne," she said.

"Sure, honey, sure," said Laverne Van Strjden, and she winked loudly. "Rely on me, Shemerelda. I won't tell a soul about Rogan Shieff. Know what I mean? Rogan Shieff! Wowee, what a catch. Sensational."

chapter nineteen

The body of Rogan Shieff was discovered at seven thirty-three next morning.

It lay on the foreshore at Beecher's Quay.

Its neck was snapped.

chapter twenty

The skink died, too.
Oh boy.

chapter twenty-one

The Tozer Tree slumbered.

Blurred gulls yawned at the morning.

Night owls dozed.

Beneath the misted waters of the broad Atlantic the salty sap coursed through the limbs of horseshoe crabs.

Ransome, the butler, descended the mellowed stone steps of the terrace and walked across the lawns to the arbor where Leonard and Shemerelda sat under vermilion parasols sipping dark and lustrous Vienna coffee.

The previous evening Leonard had returned from Venezuela.

"The death of Rogan Shieff has left me distraught," he had said.

"I am sure it has, Leonard," Shemerelda had replied.

"Did you miss me, Shemerelda?"

Shemerelda had looked up from her embroidery frame.

"Your skink is dead."

"Then, Shemerelda, we must see to its burial."

"That, Leonard, has already been attended to."

Ransome, the butler, coughed discreetly.

"Yes, Ransome?" said Leonard.

"There are two gentlemen to see madame, sir."

"I see."

"They inform me that they are members of the police department, sir."

Leonard smiled.

A damp smile.

"Have them join us, Ransome," he said. "And bring beer. I believe that is the beverage most favored by policemen. Am I right, Shemerelda?"

"I am sure you are, Leonard," said Shemerelda.

Ransome bowed his head.

A damp bow.

And he returned to the house to do his master's bidding.

Mirakel, where are you?

Mirakel, I need your broad arms to protect me.

Mirakel, I need your oak-brown thighs to straddle my resolve.

Mirakel, I need the surge of your staff to pump me with courage.

I need your sinew and the bold buck of your back.

I need your pluck in the fig-fresh gape which flickers.

Mirakel, Mirakel, I need your love.

"Lieutenant Villioressi and Detective Hawthorn, sir."

Ransome, the butler, wrinkled the tip of his nose.

"Have them sit down, Ransome," said Leonard.

Ransome motioned with a stiff inclination of his head to two straight-backed chairs.

The two detectives seated themselves in them.

"You will have beer, gentlemen?" said Leonard. "Of course you will."

Ransome, the butler, poured out two glasses of beer and on a signal from his master repaired to the house.

Snuffle of grass at his heels.

"Well then, gentlemen, and how may I assist you?" said Leonard.

Lieutenant Villioressi wiped the froth from his upper lip with the sleeve of his raincoat.

Wire-haired wrists.

Stubbled chin.

Bloodshot wince of eyes.

"Well, sir, the thing is . . . well . . ."

"Yes, Lieutenant?"

Leonard arched his eyebrows and brushed a flecklet of dust from his Manx-tweed trousers with the flat of his palm.

Lieutenant Villioressi squirmed at the pit of his chest with a nicotined forefinger.

His fallow eyes crimped at Shemerelda.

Pantaloons of Ubu lace.

Anklet of Aztec silver.

Blouse of Shantung silk.

Orange.
Loose.
Half moons of plum red nipples.
"It is your wife," he said.
"My wife?" said Leonard.
Detective Hawthorn leaned forward in his chair.
"Your wife, sir," he said. "A Mrs Tozer. We have reason to believe she can assist us in inquiries pertaining to the death of a Mr Rogan Shieff."
"Ah," said Leonard. "Ah."
Mirakel, Mirakel, where are you?
I am in danger.
I need you.
Detective Hawthorn, clumped of jaw, fine-mowed straw blond hair, stared at Shemerelda.
"Am I correct in stating, m'am, that Mr Rogan Shieff was the personal assistant to your husband?" he said.
"You are quite correct," said Leonard.
A wince of irritation.
A knotting of the jaw.
Detective Hawthorn stared harder at Shemerelda.
"Would I be right in asserting, m'am, that your relationship with Mr Rogan Shieff was of . . ."
"My wife's relationship with my former personal assistant was purely peripheral to that of my own," said Leonard.
He smiled at Detective Hawthorn.
A damp smile.
He refilled his glass.
The beer coiled and writhed.
He continued:
"My wife was in his company solely on the occasions when she visited me at my office.
"Mr Shieff did not visit us socially
"He was my servant.
"My wife's attitude towards him was totally in accordance with that status."
He smiled.
Lieutenant Villioressi sighed.
His hand fumbled in the inside pocket of his jacket.
He withdrew an envelope.
He handed it to Shemerelda.

"If what your husband says is correct, m'am," he said "perhaps you could explain this."

No tremble of Shemerelda's hand.

No flutter of cheek.

She withdrew from the envelope the dried and pressed bloom of a Tozer flower.

She withdrew a card embossed with her initials.

She looked at the writing.

Detective Hawthorn kept his eyes fixed firmly on Shemerelda's face.

"Perhaps we could trouble you to read out the inscription, Mrs Tozer," he said.

Shemerelda glanced coldly at her husband.

He smiled.

He nodded.

She read out loud:

"'I love you, darling.

"'I love you with all my heart.'"

Lieutenant Villioressi tugged softly at the lobe of his ear.

"Is that your handwriting, m'am?" he said.

"Of course," said Shemerelda.

He sighed.

He stared into the depths of his glass of beer.

"Then, maybe, m'am, you could explain what it was doing on the body of Rogan Shieff?" he said.

Mirakel, Mirakel, Mirakel.

Your staff, your thighs, your pluck.

I need them.

Shemerelda crossed her legs.

Slowly.

"I am quite unable to explain it, Lieutenant," she said. "The pressed flower, the card and its inscription were given by me to my husband.

"That is correct, is it not, Leonard?"

Leonard smiled.

A damp smile.

"Who can say, Shemerelda?" he said. "I really haven't the remotest recollection of having received them."

chapter twenty-two

Leonard, oh Leonard, what perfidy.
The damp lips of the Judas kiss.
Recreancy run riot.
What is your game, my friend?
The card embossed with Shemerelda's initials?
The loving inscription thereon?
The dried bloom of the Tozer tree?
Given to you by your wife.
Of course.
You know that.
You know that well.
The husk of the horseshoe crab croaks.
The cry of the gull dies in the throat of the muted Atlantic swell.
No wonder.
Leonard, oh Leonard, what mendacity.

chapter twenty-three

That night the blossoms of the Tozer tree coiled themselves tight against the moonlight.

Shemerelda lay naked on her bed.

She pressed her head deep into her pillow.

Her long golden hair flowed in silken eddies over the smooth curves of her back.

"Mirakel, Mirakel," she whispered softly to herself.

Hoot of owl.

Shriek of rodent.

Timid, quiverful flesh speared by heedless talons.

Gasp of startled eyes.

The burrow's warmth spiked and frosted on dead-nippled belly.

Shemerelda shivered.

The black satin sheets beneath her firm full breasts snickered as she coiled her body tight.

"Mirakel, Mirakel," she whispered.

"I remember that day well.

"Leonard was timid.

"We drove to the mansion in his car.

"It was choked by vines.

"The windows were boarded.

"Spikey grass grew through the gravel pathway.

"Slates lay splintered on the terraces.

"In the lower gardens there was a great gnarled tree.

"Its blooms were jet black.

"Leonard said:

" 'That, Shemerelda, is a Tozer tree.

" 'There is only one in the whole wide world.

" 'It was planted by my great-grandfather.

" 'It is the only thing which prospers in our family now.'

"Mirakel, Mirakel.

"My father arrived.

"He took Leonard by the arm.
"They went into the house.
"Their attornies went with them.
"I was left alone with the Tozer tree.
"I looked up into its branches.
"Mirakel, Mirakel, I surrendered myself to its blossoms.
"Sleek and black.
"I felt them pump through my veins.
"I felt them whisper at my loins.
"I cut one down from its bough.
"I placed it in my purse.
"Then my father called me from the terrace.
"I ran across to him.
"He said:
"'It is settled, Shemerelda.
"'I shall restore this mansion to its past glories.
"'It will be your dowry to Leonard.'
"Mirakel, Mirakel.
"We were married.
"We took our honeymoon in Europe.

"I saw gnarled castles and half-timbered villages. I saw paddle steamers and elvers. I saw red street-cars clanking through narrow, cobbled streets. I saw fat-fingered priests and lambs' hearts spitting on wooden skewers.

"We returned from our honeymoon.
"The mansion was restored.
"It was springtime.
"The Tozer tree bloomed deep and scarlet.
"I went to bed alone.
"I sat in my dressing room.
"I took out a card from my writing desk.
"I wrote on it these words:
"'I love you, darling.
"'I love you with all my heart.'
"I placed it in an envelope.
"I placed with it the dried black bloom of the Tozer tree.
"And I put on my wrap.
"And I walked down the landing.
"There was moonlight there.
"Leonard's bedroom door was open.
"I went in.

"He lay asleep on his bed.

"His thumb was in his mouth.

"His knees were drawn to his chest.

"Mirakel, oh Mirakel, he was so plump.

"He was pink.

"I cried.

"For a while.

"And then I placed the envelope on the table by his bed and returned to my bedroom.

"Mirakel, Mirakel, where was happiness?

"Where was bliss?

"Where was love?"

Shemerelda shivered.

Her whole body convulsed.

She tossed her long golden hair from side to side. She clawed at the pillow. She sank her teeth into it. She thrashed at the black satin sheets with her feet. Her back and her buttocks heaved.

"Mirakel, Mirakel, Mirakel."

The door of the bedroom opened.

Softly.

Shemerelda froze.

Stillness clamped her body.

"Shemerelda, Shemerelda, are you asleep?"

Leonard padded damply towards her bed.

His plump shadow fell across the whiteness of her body.

She felt its clammy weight.

She felt its clammy menace.

He placed his clammy hand on her shoulder.

"Shemerelda," he said hoarsely. "Please."

His fingers kneaded at her shoulder.

His nails bit into her flesh.

Heedless talons.

Deep inside her she heard a long lonely shriek.

"Shemerelda, please, please, please," he gasped.

She turned.

She lay on her back.

She parted her legs.

Dry husk.

He entered her.

He pumped.

'End of intercourse'

He finished.
That was all.
"Thank you, Shemerelda," he said.
Shemerelda opened her eyes.
"You are welcome, Leonard," she said.
And knuckle-tight were the blossoms of the Tozer tree.

chapter twenty-four

Shemerelda slept late.

The bee-soaked summer morning lingered among the flowers and drooled to the blossoms.

A black and white kingbird tipped its wings at an unwary fly.

A bluebird gurgled softly in a damp-shrouded arbor.

On the slender latticework of the crinkled bridge in the pagoda garden the fly catcher flicked its gray tail ceaselessly and sang.

"Phoebe, phoebe, phoe-beee," it warbled.

And Shemerelda slept on.

Oh, the gentle hills and tumbling streams of summer childhood.

The snicker of the pony's lips.

Woodsmoke from the charcoal burners' fire.

The bobcat's yarl.

Easy mist on a lazy lake.

The zirrup zirrup of the telephone woke Shemerelda.

She stretched out a drowsy arm and picked up the receiver.

"Who is this?"

"Shemerelda?"

"Yes."

"Laverne."

"Ah."

"Honey, I just gotta say it – I'm mortified. I heard the news. It kicked me right in the guts. You know? The moment I heard it, I threw up. On the spot. You're coming for lunch? Sure you are. We got some goddam fancy pasta this new Eyetalian chef has. . . . Our new chef? Honey, I clean forgot. Mr Van Strjden has engaged this new chef? And those eyes? He takes one look at me and I feel like a peeled tomato. Jesus, I look like a peeled tomato and . . ."

"Laverne?"

"Yes, honey?"

"What is this news you're referring to?"

A gasp.

The muffled clink of a glass.

"You're kidding, Shemerelda. Sure you are. You're kidding."

"No, Laverne. What is this news?"

"Why, Rogan Shieff. His death, honey. His murder."

Prickles of fear riling the scalp.

Pump of heart.

Blade of scalpel drawn in brittle whispers over nipple tip.

". . . so I waited. That's what friends are for. Sure they are. Calls of sympathy? Those you do not need. When bad news strikes, you need peace. You need calm. You need silence. Am I right? Sure I am. Okay, honey, you've had your peace. You've had your calm. You've had your silence. And now you got my sympathy. Jesus, how can you bear it? How can you sleep nights knowing your lover got his goddam neck snapped and . . ."

Hands with a free and easy tan.

A shirt of apple-green with polka dots of white.

A carnation of navy blue.

Body young and firm.

Neck snapped.

Fear.

Fear, fear, fear.

Screaming fear.

Spitting at her.

Snarling.

Screaming, screaming.

". . . and solace I can give you, honey. Comfort? Sure. A shoulder to cry on? Too damn right. But advice. Know what I mean? Advice? You need that, honey. So you ring Mr Van Strjden. This morning he tells me. Himself. Personal. 'Laverne,' he says. 'You ring Shemerelda at once, do you hear? You tell her that if she needs advice, she gotta ring me. Myself. Personal.' That's good news, Shemerelda. Mr Van Strjden is wise in these matters. He got influence in the right places. He got . . ."

And then Shemerelda saw the note on her bedside table.

It was written in Leonard's hand.

"I have to go now, Laverne," she said.
"What's that, honey?"
"Thank you for your interest. I shall call you presently."
She replaced the receiver.
She picked up the note.
Spiderwork of ink.
Backward tilt of script.
"Dear Shemerelda,
"Thank you for your participation last night.
"I found it most agreeable.
"You will be interested to know that I am to spend all day at the offices of the police department where I am to discuss matters relating to the death of my personal assistant.
"It is my wish that you should remain calm.
"I am with much love,
"Your husband,
"Leonard."
Shemerelda sprang from her bed.
The waters from the shower streamed over her urgent body and cascaded from her golden tuft.
She tossed back her hair and secured it at the nape with a clasp of slimmest Whitby jet.
Her cotton dress swirled round her naked legs as she sped down the staircase.
The sunlight smacked at the roof of the bullet-silver Bentley-Strossner as Milne, the chauffeur, simpered her to the city.
The sunlight smiled slyly on the silver statuette of the condor's head, which prowed the hood of the following black limousine.

Byrne Street.
Elevated train.
Rattle and lurch.
Canal and wharf.
Tallow factory wheezing.
Come on, train.
Come on, come on.
Clicka clacka down iron stairs.
Streetwalks aghast with heat.
Crowds.

Heaving.
Jumbling.
Jungling.
Sharp elbows. Flubber of backsides. Grinding of thighs.
Bodies rumpling, rumbling, tumbling. Bodies pressed, squashed, churned, gnashed, mauled and turmoiled.
Alcott Street.
Banners.
Bunting.
Flags.
Panting heat.
Slink of heat.
Fetid breath of heat.
The Mount Stowe Hotel.
At last. At last.
Shemerelda pushed open the swarthy door and entered the lobby.
She crossed it.
She headed for the stairs.
"Hey, lady."
Shemerelda stopped and turned.
A stout bald man in aged sweat-shirt sat behind the desk, drinking beer from a can.
"Where ya goin', lady?"
"I am going to Room Eighteen."
"No, you ain't, lady."
"I beg your pardon?"
"The guy ain't there."
"What?"
"He checked out this morning."
"What?"
"Don't keep saying 'what', lady."
"Did he leave a forwarding address?"
"Sure he did, lady. Sure he did."
"I should like to see it."
"I lost it."
"What?"
"There you go again, lady."
Shemerelda beat her fists on the desk.
She beat them hard.
She beat them rapidly.

"I must have that address," she shouted. "I must have it."

The bald stout man in the aged sweat-shirt finished his beer and lobbed the can into a cat-fested corner of the lobby.

He leaned back in his chair.

He pointed with a rumpled forefinger at Shemerelda's purse.

"There is, of course, a way I could locate it," he said.

"What?"

"Lady, will you stop saying 'what'. You're driving me bananas."

"How can you locate the . . ."

Shemerelda stopped.

She looked at the rumpled forefinger.

She looked at her purse.

"Ah," she said. "Ah, I see."

She opened her purse. She took out a twenty dollar bill. She handed it to the bald stout man.

He sniffed it.

He held it up to the light.

He stuffed it in the back pocket of his pants.

From the breast pocket of his aged sweat-shirt he took out a crumpled piece of paper.

He slid it across the desk to Shemerelda.

She snatched it.

She opened it.

Spiderwork of ink.

Backward tilt of script.

Shemerelda crashed to the floor in a blood-rushed faint.

chapter twenty-five

Another note?
In Leonard's handwriting?
In the Mount Stowe Hotel?
Oh me, oh my.
Is there no end to these twists and these turns?
Is there to be no peace?
No calm?
For chrissakes, dear reader, don't keep saying 'what'.
It's driving me bananas.

chapter twenty-six

When Shemerelda came to, she found herself lying in a pair of incredibly beautiful arms.

She looked up and found herself staring into a pair of incredibly beautiful eyes.

'Request to saints'

chapter twenty-seven

Another surprise!
The saints preserve us.
Too much.
Too much.

chapter twenty-eight

The incredibly beautiful H. H. Washbrook placed his arm around Shemerelda's waist and led her out of the lobby of the Mount Stowe Hotel.

Oh, the manliness of his mien as he steered her through the malodorous throngs.

Oh, the firmness of his step as he led her through a cool and shaded alley.

Oh, the authority of his carriage as he guided her into a street of wrought iron balconies aslung with mattresses, of smiling windows trilled by canaries, of soaring gables laughing at the clear blue sky.

And the stalls!

Dear God, rows and rows of stalls set out in the middle of the crooked street.

Stalls selling paper hats.

Stalls selling candy and streamers, dolls and balloons.

Stalls selling food.

And what food!

A positive prodigality of exotic provender.

Salamanders roasted on skewers.

Sauces glop glopping.

Stews slob slobbing.

Limpets, crayfish, scallops, whelks.

Lamb fries, headcheese, pigs' knuckles, fricandeau, calves' brains.

Macaroni, fagioli, lasagne, spaghetti, vermicelli.

Terrapins poached in their shells.

An opulence of galactose and glycogen.

An amplitude of ichthulin and protamine.

The incredibly beautiful H. H. Washbrook took Shemerelda by the hand and gently drew her through a bead curtained doorway.

The beads chuckled softly on their cords.

They stood in a stone-flagged courtyard shielded from the sky by the fronds of palms.

A nymph-bound fountain creamed and gurgled.

There were slender-legged tables with red and white check tablecloths.

A slender waiter with sleeked-black hair and a cast in his eye came to greet them.

"Signor Washbrook," he said as he guided them to a flower-decked alcove. "What pleasure. What honor."

"Bring us wine, Luigi," said the incredibly beautiful H. H. Washbrook, and he drew back a wicker chair and seated Shemerelda therein.

The wine was cool.

It was tangy.

It was joyous to the tongue.

"You are feeling better, Shemerelda?" said the incredibly beautiful H. H. Washbrook.

Shemerelda closed her eyes.

"Thank you. Yes," she said.

A mandolin played.

A tenor sang.

Peace.

Perfection.

Shemerelda raised the lids of her eyes flimsily and gazed at the incredibly beautiful man who sat before her.

What confidence of manner.

What elegance of clothes.

What refinement of features.

She opened her eyes wide.

"I have to ask you something, Mr Washbrook," she said.

"Please do."

"You found me in the lobby of the Mount Stowe Hotel."

"Yes."

"What were you doing there?"

The incredibly beautiful H. H. Washbrook chuckled.

"I could well ask you the same question, Shemerelda," he said.

She felt a blushlet rising to her cheeks.

Prickles of fear once more.

Fool.

What an idiot she was.

Her secret had been uncovered.

She had no lie to come padding obediently to her tongue.

She tried to suppress her fluster.

The incredibly beautiful H. H. Washbrook smiled and rested an incredibly beautiful hand on her forearm.

Oh, the bliss of that touch.

"Relax, Shemerelda," he said. "Sit back and enjoy the festival."

"The festival?" she said eager to corral her indiscretions out of harm.

"The Festival of Santa Carlotta," said the incredibly beautiful H. H. Washbrook. "Let me explain."

He spoke with calm, measured tones, but his voice lilted to the roll and rill of Tuscan hillside, sang to the rhythm of Roman breezes, whispered to the soft chatter of alpine becks, as he told her of the humble peasant girl who had seen the vision of Christ on the udder of her goat, who had heard the voice of Holy Mary in the croak of her gander, who had crossed the wide Atlantic from her native Italy, who had tended to the sick and poor in the fleshpots of Rackham City, who had died beneath the wheels of an errant streetcar and whose birth was this day being celebrated with joy, with laughter and with tears.

Shemerelda was bewitched.

How beautiful he was.

How urbane.

No, no, no.

What was he doing in the Mount Stowe Hotel?

Why had he . . .

Those incredibly beautiful eyes.

Those exquisitely shaped ears.

That square and dimpled chin.

No, no, no.

He was a threat.

He was danger.

He was . . .

How wonderful to lie abed in those arms.

How unbearably, ravenously, overpoweringly delicious to feel those hands caressing the secret eddies of her body.

How sensuous to . . .

Mirakel, Mirakel, Mirakel.

The note!
Where was the note?
She scrambled her hands in her purse.
She threw out its contents onto the red and white check tablecloth.
There was no note.
No note!
Where was the note?
"Mr Washbrook," she said sharply.
"Yes, Shemerelda," said her companion, raising a gracefully arched eyebrow.
"When you found me, did you by any chance see a note?"
"A note, Shemerelda?"
"A note. I had it in my hand. The desk clerk gave it me. I paid him twenty dollars. He gave me this note. I was holding it when I fainted. You must have seen it. You must have seen that note."
The incredibly beautiful H. H. Washbrook stretched out his legs and rested his hands upon the back of his neck.
He smiled.
Oh, that smile.
He shook his head slowly.
"No, Shemerelda," he said firmly. "I saw no note."
He took her by the arm.
He led her outside.
He seated her in the rear seat of the black limousine.
He sat beside her.
Oh, the propinquity.
The black limousine drew up outside the vine-encrusted mansion.
He declined her invitation to take tea.
Oh, the propriety.
As the black limousine turned on the gravel driveway Shemerelda paused at the door.
She looked back.
And she saw it
She saw the silver statuette of the condor's head.

chapter twenty-nine

Who is this arsehole, H. H. Washbrook?
Arrogant swine.
How dare he intrude on Shemerelda's happiness.
What effrontery.
The hauteur of his behavior.
The fanfaronade.
The vanity and the conceit.
The man is a turd.

chapter thirty

The nights are long.

They yearn.

They ache.

Mirakel, where are you?

Mirakel, I need you.

Shemerelda tossed and turned in her bed.

The condor's head.

Of course, of course.

It was the limousine with the condor's head which had tried to force her off the Old Smugglers' Highway.

But why?

Why should the incredibly beautiful H. H. Washbrook wish to harm her?

Was it coincidence that brought him to her swoon in the lobby of the Mount Stowe Hotel?

If not, why was he there?

The long, hot summer nights, sweet with the scents of honeysuckle, frizzed with the chirps of cricket, hunted by owl and high-pitched bat, howled in the hollow eaves of Shemerelda's mind.

Mirakel, Mirakel.

The note!

Why?

Why had Leonard written the note?

What was his association with Mirakel?

Did he know of her association with Mirakel?

Did he know how she yelled and heaved and clawed at the height of her passion?

Did he know of the soft and gentle lap of her tongue?

Did he know of breasts swaying, backs arching, legs entwining?

Mirakel, Mirakel, where are you?

Shemerelda prowled around her bedroom.

Sway of drapes in night breeze.
Blink and beat of jet plane.
Salt-crusted croak of timber-laden tramp.
The two detectives.
Wire-haired wrists.
Straw-blond hair.
What had Leonard revealed to them?
What lies had he told?
Why had he betrayed her?
The card was written to him.
He knew that.
The dried bloom of the Tozer tree was given to him.
He knew that.
Why deny it?
Why, why, why?
Shemerelda flung herself upon her bed.

The hot sheets writhed into her body. The pillow knuckled at her chin. She screamed loud and long into its downy depths.

But of her distress during the night Shemerelda gave no indication during the day.

How calm she was.

How cool.

How correct.

"I trust you slept well last night, Shemerelda," said Leonard.

"Extremely well, Leonard, thank you."

How solicitous he was when he returned home from work.

"I trust you had a pleasant day, Shemerelda."

"Extremely pleasant, thank you, Leonard."

How attentive he was.

"Are you wanting for anything, Shemerelda?"

"Nothing at all, thank you, Leonard."

And she turned to her slim volume of the pensées of Gerhardt Gefunden.

The scarlet blossoms of the Tozer tree were fading fast in the blazing heat of summer.

Dry, crackling petals.

Scarlet blistered by the sun, drooping pink and brown.

Yet one blossom remained.

It stood up straight and proud from its bough.

'Blossom vandalism'

A flag of scarlet, erect and potent.

After a long and sleepless night Shemerelda walked to the lower gardens and placed herself in front of the Tozer tree.

She stared at the single scarlet blossom.

She ran the moist tip of her tongue softly round the rim of her lips.

Slowly she parted the loose folds of her blouse and revealed her firm young breasts.

She reached out for the blossom.

Firm it was in her hand.

Throbbing to her touch.

Pulsing.

Straining.

With a sudden violent movement of her wrist she snapped the blossom off its bough.

She crumpled it in the palm of her hand.

She ground it between her fingers.

She flung it high into the summer breeze.

And with a sigh she fell to her knees and sobbed.

From the upstairs window of his bedroom Leonard watched her.

And a smile spread with a smug purr across his face.

chapter thirty-one

"You have been somewhat out of sorts these past few days, Shemerelda," said Leonard as they took breakfast on the upper patio.

"Ah," said Shemerelda.

The terra cotta pots and urns were rampaged by petunias, cascaded by lobelias and parasoled by lilies of darkest green and gold.

Above the cool roll of the lawns a black and orange redstart flitted.

Then it dropped its wings and fanned its tail.

The Flensberg china tea cups clinked.

"I should like you to join me on an outing today, Shemerelda."

"Ah."

"It is the day of the car race."

"I see."

"I shall be competing, of course."

"Ah."

"Will you accompany me, Shemerelda?"

Shemerelda clasped her hands tightly beneath the table.

"If that is what you wish," she said.

"It is," said Leonard.

The car race.

Wowee!

On the broad strands adjoining the South Rackhamshire Croquet and Real Tennis Club.

My, oh my.

The cream of the cream of Rackham City society was out in force.

"You hear the speech last night?"

"Nope."

"You didn't hear the speech last night?"
"Nope."
"I heard the speech last night. It sure was good."
In the paddock carved in the tawny flanks of the dunes the sports cars stallioned themselves in gleaming rows.
Bradwell Specials with snarling fenders.
Lutz-Peugeots from France. Bugattis from Italy. Porsches from Germany. Aston Martins from England. And from the good old USA the Jackson-Bonnevilles and the Tobias Flyers.
What a sneering of chrome.
What a scowling of brass.
Whine, winge, shriek and deep-bellied growl.
Stench of gas and burning rubber.
Strident clash of colour.
Indathrene blue and hellebore red, sunflower yellow and meadow brook green, chrome primrose and cinder gray, magenta, nigrosine and oriole.
And how the drivers peacocked and preened.
What a slapping of thighs, a twirling of cravats, a posing, a posturing.
"What a load of jerks."
Laverne Van Strjden flared her nostrils.
"I need liquor," she said. "Let's go, Shemerelda."
Shemerelda followed Laverne Van Strjden as she strode briskly through the idlers on the croquet lawn.
They entered the ladies' withdrawing room and Laverne Van Strjden summoned the waiter with a staccato click of the fingers.
"Scotch for me. And for you, Shemerelda?"
"Cassis, if you please."
"What in the name of shit's that?"
Shemerelda smiled.
"It is a French drink, Laverne. Quite delicious."
"Sure it is, honey. Sure it is."
Laverne Van Strjden took out her compact and mortared powder on her eagline nose with a galumphing puff.
She snapped her compact shut and downed her scotch in a single gulp.
"Well, well, well, Shemerelda," she said. "You sure do look sensational."

"Thank you, Laverne."

Shemerelda ran her thumb down the spoke-sharp creases of her Lhasa linen slacks.

She gently fingered the cool white collar of her Kendal cotton shirt.

"Will you just look at me," said Laverne Van Strjden. "I look like the chutney tray in a goddam Indian restaurant."

She ordered another glass of scotch as Shemerelda slowly sipped her cassis.

Then she said earnestly:

"Don't give up, honey."

"I beg your pardon, Laverne?"

"Okay, your lover's dead. Tough. So get yourself another. Know what I mean? Sure you do."

Mirakel, Mirakel.

My mouth hungers for you.

It gapes for your juices.

". . . got himself awfully mangled in an automobile accident in St Louis. So what did I do? I took his brother. Did I ever tell you about that dum dum? I didn't. I'll tell you now. What a body. What an appetite in bed. Bed? We never got to bed he was so goddam eager for it. At the back of the school locker room. In his father's pick-up. At the top of . . ."

A bedroom simple and austere.

A table.

A chair.

A bed.

Mirakel, Mirakel.

". . . so listen real careful. Mr Van Strjden? He got these two new assistants. Wow! Honey, you and me could play real groovy music with them. Know what I mean? Sure you do. Danes. Twin brothers. Bodies like Greek Gods. Just ready and eager for the plucking. You leave it all to me. Know what I mean? Sure you do. Next Thursday Mr Van Strjden flies to Seattle, so what I'll do is I'll . . ."

Seattle.

The train trip there with grandmother.

Idaho potatoes.

Yellowstone River.

Windows misted by Rockies' mountain chill.

World's Fair.

Space needle.
Soaring strong and vibrant, thrusting, thrusting at the yielding sky.
Mirakel, Mirakel, Mirakel.
"You're in trouble, Shemerelda."
"What?"
Shemerelda started.
Her heart pumped.
The palms of her hand clammed.
"You got big trouble, honey. Am I right? Sure I am."
Laverne Van Strjden's gaze bored deep into her.
It splintered inner fibre and shredded secret nerve end.
"I know these things, kid. I'm a witch. Well, with looks like mine what else could I be?"
She leaned forwards across the table.
Sour croak of scotch upon her breath.
Spiky motes of powder upon her eagline nose.
"I look at you, Shemerelda, and I see fear. I see terror."
The calm, dark inner mirror turned opaque and across its surface ran a snickering, jagged crack.
"No one else sees it. Outside you're the same Shemerelda. Beautiful. Cool. Serene. But I see underneath the fabric, kid. And what do I see? I see fear. I see terror."
She threw back her head and laughed.
Vulpine howl.
Flash of gold on teeth.
Carpet of must on tongue.
"You need help, honey. You ring Mr Van Strjden. Know what I mean? Sure you do."
Shemerelda stood up.
"I must go, Laverne," she said. "It is time for the first race."
"Oh that," said Laverne Van Strjden. "A load of crap. Horny cars driven by guys with limp front fenders."
Shemerelda left Laverne Van Strjden to her seventh glass of scotch and stepped out into the postprandial sunlight.

On her way to the paddock Shemerelda was greeted by Admiral and Mrs Kolokof.
The aged salt tipped the peak of an aged sea cap, and his consort fluttered her aged eyelids.
Mr Edwin Culpepper, the noted toxicologist, touched his

sandy forelock, and his angular fiancée, Clovissa, let loose an angular titter.

In the shade of a somnolent cedar tree Mr Van Strjden played bridge with Mr Ikin, Mr Stollmeyer and Mr Norse.

They rose to their feet as Shemerelda passed by, and Mr Van Strjden doffed his panama.

Shemerelda found Leonard leaning on the leather-strapped hood of his crimson Bradwell-Special.

His face was white.

Globes of perspiration stood out on his brow.

His forearms trembled.

"What is the matter, Leonard?" said Shemerelda.

Leonard shook his head, and a trickle of green bile ran down his chin.

"The master refuses to drive, madam," said Milne, the chauffeur.

He was dressed in dungarees of navy blue.

On his cheeks were stains of grease.

"However, madam, allow me to rectify the matter forthwith," he said with a courteous nod of the head.

And he took Leonard roughly by the shoulders and snarled:

"Get in, you yellow bastard. And drive."

He lifted up Leonard by the scruff of the neck, stuffed him into the driver's seat and cuffed him violently several times on the head with the back of his hand.

Leonard winced, and then with a roar, a screech and a puff of ink-blue smoke the crimson Bradwell-Special bucked its way to the starting grid.

Milne, the chauffeur, wiped his hands on the seat of his dungarees.

"My apologies, madam, for the indiscreet language," he said.

"That is quite in order, Milne," said Shemerelda. "Let us hope the yellow bastard is victorious."

He was.

chapter thirty-two

"Your husband drove a fine race, Mrs Tozer."

Shemerelda, sipping cassis in the shade of the somnolent cedar tree, looked up to see the incredibly beautiful H. H. Washbrook surveying her with his incredibly beautiful smile.

He was dressed in leathers of purest doe-skin.

Around his neck was a scarf of finest Hawkwood chambray.

The polo neck of a deep mauve Kelso cashmere sweater peeked above the black silk collar of his leathers.

"Perhaps I may join you after my race, Mrs Tozer," he said.

"You may," said Shemerelda.

"I wish you success, Mr Washbrook," said Mr Van Strjden.

"Thank you, Mr Van Strjden," said the incredibly beautiful H. H. Washbrook. Then he turned to Shemerelda and said: "Wish me luck, Mrs Tozer. It would be most enjoyable to do battle with your husband in the Grand Finale."

Shemerelda nodded her head slowly.

"I wish you luck, Mr Washbrook," she said.

Distant roar of automobile.

Distant slur and slough of spectators.

It was cool under the cedar tree.

Slick and slide of cards on table.

From time to time Mr Van Strjden smiled at Shemerelda.

High-pitched yaffle of distant racers.

Low-pitched moans of distant spectators.

Distant boom of loudspeakered commentator.

"And on Lap Sixteen.

"In the lead.

"It's . . .

"Number Thirty-two, Jarvey Murdoch in his Maserati.

"Then it's . . .

"Number Eight, Tony Kustow in his Laryea-Allen.

"Then it's . . .

"Number Seventeen, H. H. Washbrook in his . . ."

The bridge game was concluded.

Mr Ikin, Mr Stollmeyer and Mr Norse paid their respects to Shemerelda and left the table.

Mr Van Strjden ordered a pot of Hitchcock and Throwley prime darjeeling and poured out a cup of that rich and fulvous aromatic tea for Shemerelda.

"And coming into the Lighthouse chicane.

"It's . . .

"Still.

"Number Thirty-two, Jarvey Murdoch in his Maserati.

"And challenging hard.

"It's . . .

"The Diatto-Tipo of H. H. Washbrook.

"He's followed.

"By . . .

"Number Nineteen, Clive Bell in his Woolf-Hellcat.

"He's followed.

"By . . .

"Number Twenty-eight, Art Poniatowski in his . . ."

Mr Van Strjden sighed.

"Such a wearisome sport, don't you think, Shemerelda?" he said.

"Yes, I do," said Shemerelda.

Mr Van Strjden gently swirled the ambrosial beverage in the bottom of his cup.

Sweet fragrance.

"Some time ago, Shemerelda, we had a little chat, you and I," he said.

"Yes," said Shemerelda.

"I told you about a certain clandestine relationship I had established with a young woman many years ago."

"Yes," said Shemerelda.

Mr Van Strjden made a slight adjustment to the brim of his panama.

"I feel that you are in need of help, Shemerelda," he said.

Shemerelda stared at him.

Unblinkingly.

"I am in a position to give you that help, my dear."

Shemerelda stared at him.

Unblinkingly.

He took out a pocket notebook bound in maroon Stockholm leather.

He wrote in it. He detached the page. He folded it neatly. He leaned across the table and took Shemerelda's purse. He opened it. He placed inside the neatly folded note. He closed it. He pushed it back across the table to Shemerelda.

He smiled.

"You will find a private telephone number written on my note, Shemerelda," he said. "I am sure it will not be long before you make contact with me."

And he doffed his panama hat and left Shemerelda alone beneath the somnolent cedar tree.

"And.

"Crossing the winning line.

"It's.

"Number Seventeen, H. H. Washbrook in his Diatto-Tipo.

"He's followed.

"By.

"Number Thirty-two, Jarvey Murdoch in his . . ."

Laverne Van Strjden weaved her way to the table and sat down heavily opposite Shemerelda.

"H. H. Washbrook. Wowee! Know what I mean, honey? Sure you do. Sure."

The grand finale.

Sun-split strand.

Sea ashimmer.

High circle of gulls.

Stoop and plop of tern.

"And, ladies and gentlemen, very shortly the competitors will be lining up on the starting grid for the commencement of the Grand Finale race.

"And, ladies and gentlemen, the competitors.

"Are.

"Number Two, Micky Meisel in his Loman-Miller Special.

"And.

"Number Five, Leonard Tozer in his . . ."

Shemerelda found Leonard in his transporter-trailer.

He was throwing up.

Milne, the chauffeur, stood over him.

"You got to, you bastard. You got to," he shouted.

"No," said Leonard. "I can't."

"What is amiss, Milne?" said Shemerelda.

"The master refuses to race, madam," said Milne, the chauffeur.

And then he turned to Leonard, took hold of the collar of his leathers, shook him and shouted:

"You're yellow. You got no more guts than a toothless chihuahua. Yellow bastard. Yellow, yellow, yellow."

Leonard slumped to the floor.

Vomit encrusted his chin.

His eyes watered.

"I order you to obey me," he said.

"No way," screamed Milne, the chauffeur.

"I order you to drive in my place," said Leonard.

And then he rolled himself into a ball as Milne, the chauffeur, lashed out at him with his foot.

Shemerelda stood in the doorway of the transporter-trailer.

White calm of Kendal cotton shirt.

Whimper of Leonard.

Husky rasp of Milne, the chauffeur.

"Milne," said Shemerelda softly.

"Yes, madam?"

"I order you to do as your master bids."

"Certainly, madam."

He dragged Leonard to his feet.

He ripped off his racing leathers.

He rammed them over the top of his dungarees.

He fastened the racing helmet over his head.

He pulled down the goggles over his eyes.

But before he wrapped the fireproof scarf around his mouth he snarled:

"Okay, wise guy. But when it's over, you ask me. Right? You ask me about the Byrne Street El. Right? You ask me about the trip I made there with your wife. Got it? Got it, you yellow bastard?"

He aimed another kick at Leonard.

And then he affixed the fireproof scarf across his mouth and bowed to Shemerelda.

"I am ready to oblige, madam," he said.

Shemerelda smiled.

"Thank you, Milne," she said.

She turned to Leonard, crunched in the corner of the transporter-trailer among the tyres and the jacks.

"I shall lock the door behind me, Leonard," she said. "Cower away, my sweet. Cower away."

The sports cars assembled in the paddock.

The incredibly beautiful H. H. Washbrook waved an incredibly beautiful gloved hand at Shemerelda.

She nodded her head in acknowledgement.

Milne, the chauffeur, clambered into the driving seat of the crimson Bradwell-Special.

He beckoned to Shemerelda.

And above the engine's shark-throated tatter he shouted:

"Okay, honey, give me a kiss. And make it for real."

"Certainly," said Shemerelda.

She leaned forward.

She pressed her lips tight to his mouth.

She burrowed her breasts deep into his chest.

She placed her hand in his groin and softly squeezed.

"Jeee-sus," said Milne, the chauffeur.

"Good luck, Leonard," she said in a loud voice as she withdrew herself from the cab of the car. "Good luck, my darling."

She repaired to the pits.

Behind her in the transporter-trailer Leonard retched once more.

The sports cars strained clamorously at the starting grid.

Quiver and shiver.

Roar and rumble.

Blare and blast.

Scatter of gulls.

Shriek of terns.

And then she saw him.

No doubt about it.

He was in the PS Tatra horizontally-opposed, two-cylinder, overhead-valve with the swing axle front.

Mirakel.

No mistaking the set of the shoulders.

No mistaking the muscled squat of the neck.

He caught her eye.

He nodded.

She sensed the smile that spread beneath the fireproof scarf, and her loins ached and her tongue darted.

"Mirakel, Mirakel, Mirakel," she shouted.

But her voice was drowned by the sky-cracking clangor as the cars leapt forward to the drop of the starter's flag.

chapter thirty-three

Milne's funeral pyre was most spectacular.

Shemerelda watched it in slow-motion horror.

Lap One.

The Tatra affixed itself firmly behind the crimson Bradwell-Special.

At the Lighthouse chicane it nudged the offside rear wheel of the crimson Bradwell-Special.

Snake of car.

Screech of brakes.

Milne grappled with the wheel.

Feverishly.

In the Clubhouse straight the Tatra drew alongside the crimson Bradwell-Special and gently nuzzled it with its flanks.

"And we have trouble.

"Number Five, Leonard Tozer struggles to keep control.

"Yes, sir, he's fighting the wheel.

"He's . . .

"Wowee.

"He's done it.

"Sure thing.

"He's back on the track, ladies and gentlemen.

"He's back in the race."

Lap Three.

Side by side raced the crimson Bradwell-Special and the silver Tatra.

The approach to Rockpool Corner.

Side by side. Full speed. Flat out.

Who would yield?

Onwards, onwards.

Nearer and nearer.

Too late.

The crimson Bradwell-Special hurtled into the air in a plume of sand and smoke.

Over it turned in the sun-silked air.

Once.

Twice.

Thrice.

And then it descended to the clenched rocks in a jangle and clatter of searing sparks.

Silence.

A mere flicklet of silence.

And then the explosion.

An ochre-hearted vomit of sound that flung back the full-bellied surf of the broad Atlantic.

Flickering sheets of white and primrose.

A slow and solemn column of jet-black smoke.

And in the distance, hazed by the heat and dappled by the shimmer of the sea, the silver Tatra sped away and out of sight.

chapter thirty-four

Do it now, Shemerelda.
There is no time to lose.
Call Mr Van Strjden.
Pick up that receiver.
Press those buttons.
Speak.
Now.
"Mr Van Strjden?"
"Of course."
"This is Shemerelda."
"Of course."
"I wish to see you."
"Of course."
There.
The deed is done.
No need to change.
You look superb.
Go.
Now.
Brave Shemerelda.
Beautiful, beautiful Shemerelda.
Go now.

chapter thirty-five

In the high roosts of Ocean Heights Mr Van Strjden has his secret lair.

He waits for Shemerelda.

The sheets in his bedroom are pure and unsullied.

The mirrored ceiling lusters.

On the mauve-draped walls there is but one picture.

A print.

A full-juiced fig.

Ripe.

Gaping wide.

Mr Van Strjden nods and smiles.

He crossed the glass-tiled lobby.

The soft-soled Goanese steward places his arms across his chest and bends forwards from the hips.

Mr Van Strjden smiles and nods.

He pauses before the gilded cage.

The conure defecates.

The Burma cat impales its breast with cold and motionless eyes.

Mr Van Strjden nods and smiles.

He enters the drawing room.

No oriental rugs.

No fabrics from the East.

Walls bound in skins from the Cape.

A ceiling, slightly coved, in Morocco of nasturtium-red.

Mouldings and plinths indigo-lacquered.

Ebony bookshelves.

Skins of tiger and fox fur strewn on the floor.

A money changer's table, a church lectern of wrought iron, a singing desk.

Windows of crackle glass and bottle-punt dressed with drapes cut from ecclesiastical stoles.

'Byzantine monstrances'

A chimney piece dressed in Florentine silk, flanked by Byzantine monstrances of gilded copper.

And in its centre a triptych with lace-work panels.

Mr Van Strjden surveys it all, and he is well-pleased.

The door bell whispers.

A pause.

The moth-foot steward bows.

A young woman in the full-juiced bloom of her beauty enters the drawing room.

"Shemerelda, my dear," says Mr Van Strjden. "All is ready."

chapter thirty-six

Shemerelda reclined on a blue fox fur.

The reflected nasturtium-red of the ceiling smouldered in her cool, dark clefting.

Mr Van Strjden, minute and middle-aged and rich as well, stood at the singing desk.

He smiled.

He nodded.

He spoke.

"How beautiful you look, Shemerelda.

"How ill you would have been suited by widow's weeds."

Not a flicker from Shemerelda's eyes.

"We were all so relieved, Shemerelda, that it was not your husband who was killed in that most distressing automobile accident.

"How awful to learn that it was his chauffeur who had spiked his drink in order that he might himself compete in the race.

"The perfidy of servants these days, my dear."

Not a flicker from Shemerelda's eyes.

Mr Van Strjden smiled and nodded.

"I have to tell you now, Shemerelda, that you will no longer be troubled by the police."

Not a flicker from Shemerelda's eyes.

"I have influence. I have money. I have used both."

The Burma cat strutted, stiff-legged, into the room.

It affixed Shemerelda with cold and motionless eyes.

It yawned.

Mr Van Strjden smiled.

He leaned forward across the singing desk.

"Shemerelda," he said. "It was I who arranged the murder of Rogan Shieff."

Shemerelda affixed him with cold, motionless eyes.

Her anklet of Aztec silver glowered in the flicker of the Yalta candles.

"I received information that he had purloined a note from your husband. I am instructed that he intended to use it in the most dishonorable manner."

The Burma cat stilted out of the room, swishing its tail from side to side.

"It was his intention to maintain that you had written the note to him. If your husband denied it, he intended to reveal certain matters of a business nature which could have proved most embarrassing to what we know as 'the Tozer Empire'."

A fleck of spittle appeared on his lower lip.

"If your husband did not deny it, then Mr Shieff would have felt free to have compelled you to become his lover."

Not a stir from Shemerelda's eyes.

"Ah, Shemerelda, the sacrifices young women will make to maintain the integrity of their husbands."

Mr Van Strjden sighed.

"A most disagreeable business.

"It was best to be rid of him."

The Goanese steward flimpered across the rugs and furs and offered Shemerelda a cup of mocha.

She declined.

Mr Van Strjden smiled and nodded.

"Shemerelda," he said. "You are an extremely wealthy young woman. I am pleased to note that your wealth has been kept entirely separate from the financial affairs of your husband.

"Very wise.

"You see, my dear, I have to tell you that your husband's 'empire' is on the verge of ruin.

"Total collapse.

"Most sad.

"Most distressing.

"My only consolation is that your financial circumstances will not be affected by your husband's downfall and disgrace."

Still not a flicker from Shemerelda's eyes.

Still the deep, brooding smoulder in the cleft of her breasts.

Still the arched-white smoothness of her neck.

Still the silkiness of her long blonde hair.

"Your husband's attempts to extricate himself from his

difficulties are causing me much concern, Shemerelda.

"I am particularly distressed at his choice of associates."

He leaned forward once more across the singing desk.

He narrowed his eyes.

"His closest associate, Shemerelda, is known by the name, Mirakel."

Silence.

Flicker of candle.

Glow of nasturtium-red.

Glint of bottle-punt.

"I believe you are acquainted with him, Shemerelda."

He laughed.

What a dry cackle.

"I know you are acquainted with him, Shemerelda.

"I know, too, it is your dearest wish to discover his whereabouts.

"I have that information. Shemerelda.

"I am prepared to pass it on to you.

"For a consideration."

Mr Van Strjden smiled.

He nodded.

He spoke:

"I shall tell you where Mirakel is to be found if you will agree to become my lover."

Shemerelda stood up.

"Certainly," she said. "Is now convenient?"

chapter thirty-seven

Mr Van Strjden leads Shemerelda to the door of his apartment.

He holds her lightly by the wrist.

His eyes gleam.

His skin shimmers.

"Thank you, Shemerelda," he says. "Thank you so much."

The Goanese steward bows and opens the door.

"There is one more thing, Shemerelda," says Mr Van Strjden.

"Yes?"

"You might like to know who was responsible for the death of Mr Rogan Shieff."

"Might I?"

"Oh yes. Oh yes, Shemerelda," he says.

He nods.

He giggles.

He speaks.

"You see, he really is the most incredibly beautiful man."

She leaves the apartment.

chapter thirty-eight

Another shock!

Is there no end to them?

Rogan Shieff's demise.

Leonard's distress.

Mirakel, Mirakel, Mirakel.

What next?

Has Shemerelda really given her full-juiced young body to the minute bon vivant and epicure?

Do sheets lie arumpled, impure and sullied?

Does the mirrored ceiling hug to itself dark and carnal secrets?

No.

Rest easy.

The conure remains impassive.

The Burma cat refuses its master's knee.

The Goanese steward snores with content in the pantry.

Mr Van Strjden is not yet ready for the quenching of the heart's immortal thirst.

Hold on, though.

Let us not get carried away.

Let us be absolutely certain we know where we stand.

Here is a check list:

Concentrate.

Leonard's business faces ruin?

Right.

Leonard and Mirakel are involved in dubious association?

Right.

Leonard has betrayed Shemerelda?

Right.

Mr Van Strjden arranged for the murder of Rogan Shieff, knows the whereabouts of Mirakel and wishes to enter an adulterous relationship with Shemerelda?

Right.

'End of irritating interlude'

The incredibly beautiful H. H. Washbrook murdered Rogan Shieff?

Did he?

Could such a man have stooped to such baseness?

Let us not commit ourselves to hasty judgment.

Let us await developments.

Meanwhile the story continues.

Apace.

chapter thirty-nine

The day of the Governor's Ball.

Wowee!

The cream of the cream of Rackham City society is aflutter with anticipation.

Whales cavort in the Downey River.

Songbirds trill.

Horseshoe crabs lumber shorewards.

The Tozer tree is bare of blossom.

Naked.

It is three days since Shemerelda's visit to the high roosts of Ocean Heights.

In mid-morning Shemerelda plunged into the pool.

Her naked body flensed through the fronds of crystal clear water.

The lissom stroke of arms.

The curve of back.

The sleek of thighs.

She plunged.

She twisted.

She floated.

And high above her a skein of wild duck flew high to the distant hills of her childhood.

She closed her eyes.

Ah, sweet memories.

She saw tumbling mountain streams.

She heard the woodsaw's whine.

She heard the buoyant click of her grandfather's cork leg and heard the whinny of Appaloosa and Morgan.

She saw innocence.

Simplicity.

Bliss.

Calm and order.

When she opened her eyes, she saw Leonard standing at the pool's edge.

He was staring down at her.

He wore white bell-bottom linen slacks and a gansey of navy blue.

She swam to the side and, ignoring Leonard's helping hand, hauled herself lightly out of the water.

Her nipples, taut and erect, stretched out to the sun.

Her firm full breasts heaved calmly.

She lay back on a Quetzoc divan and soothed her hand upon her golden thicket.

Leonard sat down beside her.

"I am looking forward keenly to the Governor's Ball tonight, Shemerelda," he said.

"Ah," said Shemerelda.

"We must throw a ball ourselves.

"In the fall.

"Yes, the fall would be admirable.

"We shall spare no expense. The finest foods. The finest wines. The finest spirits. The finest orchestras. And you, Shemerelda, shall be decked in the finest of gowns."

"Thank you," said Shemerelda.

Leonard left his chair and knelt by her side.

He placed his hand on her belly.

He squeezed.

"We must extend ourselves, Shemerelda.

"Money is no object.

"A world cruise. Yes. A world cruise. After the ball we shall go on a world cruise. And when we return, we shall completely refurbish our home.

"Choice pieces of furniture from France. Sumptuous carpets from the East. We shall employ the best interior decorator in the whole of the United States and our home will dazzle with its splendour and its magnificence.

"And something else.

"We shall completely re-landscape the gardens.

"We shall have a grotto. And formal parkland with rare breeds of sheep and cattle. And we shall plant exotic trees from all quarters of the world.

"We must extend ourselves, Shemerelda.

"Money is no object."

Shemerelda closed her eyes once more.

Her husband's hand remained upon her belly.

Damply.

The sun unfolded the petals of her memory and burst them into bloom.

Her wedding day.

Marquees on the lawn.

Black musicians in white tuxedos.

Peacocks with collars of diamonds and rubies.

Her father placed his arm around her waist.

He spoke.

– Shemerelda, I hope you are happy right now.

– Indeed I do.

– But whatever your feelings, my darling, you must always remember that you are a very wealthy young woman.

She nodded.

– And when I die, you will be even wealthier. Will you keep that very firmly in your mind?

She nodded.

– But most of all, my dearest darling, I want you to remember that all this wealth is yours and yours alone.

– Will you promise me that it shall always remain so?

She nodded.

– No one else shall ever touch your wealth.

– No one.

He paused.

He spun Shemerelda around to face him.

He stared down into her eyes.

– I hope your husband understands that well, Shemerelda.

– Indeed I do.

She nodded.

Memories!

Ah, how sweet, how bitter.

A small purple-veined cloud crossed the sun.

Its shadow passed over Shemerelda's lids, and she opened her eyes.

Leonard was gazing at her intently.

"There is so much we have to do with our lives, Shemerelda," he said.

"My enterprises flourish.

"Did I tell you about my airship?

"My associates and I have invested vast sums of money in a revolutionary new airship design.

"We have the prototype completed.

"Shemerelda, it will be the most colossal success.

"South America? Wide open for airship transport. Crying out for it. Begging for it. That is why I was in Venezuela. Setting up deals. Setting up deals, my precious Shemerelda, which will bring us a fortune so incalculable we shall . . . we shall . . ."

He snatched up Shemerelda from the Quetzoc divan and kissed her full on the lips.

She did not flinch.

"Oh, Shemerelda, how my enterprises flourish.

"The money simply pours in."

chapter forty

The evening of the Governor's Ball.

Claret glow of dying sun.

Soft patter of wild duck on tidal creek.

Dolphin's leap.

Shemerelda sat in her dressing room in front of her mirror.

Her dress was unadorned by flower or jewel.

She slipped off her shoulder straps and let it fall to her waist.

Her breasts stood out firm and full.

Leonard trod softly up behind her and gently powdered the tips of her plum-red nipples.

He pressed his mouth into her neck.

He cupped her breasts in his hands and stroked their proud shimmering flanks.

He pressed his loins into the pit of her naked back.

"Shall we, Shemerelda?" he whispered. "Shall we? Please. Please."

Shemerelda turned to him.

She smiled.

She hooked up her shoulder straps.

That was all.

The limousines and landaus, beetle-sleek and vain, processed to the Governor's Ball.

It was to be held on the *Queen Carolina*.

Oh, noble liner.

Oh, proud temptress of the windy seas, oh, beguiling siren of the tropic oceans, oh, swift huntress of spice-scented isles, what straits to be in now.

Moored to the quay at Cocker's Point.

No more to roam.

No wind-lashed rigging. No melon moon on mainmast top. No prancing waves at prow. No dip of ensign to warship's pass. No furies to fight. No calms to seduce.

Tethered now by hawsers.

Fettered.

Gyved and hoppled.

Dolphin turned to cow.

"What a stunning vision," said Leonard to Shemerelda as they stepped out of the new Lagonda-Europa.

Shemerelda looked up at the proud shimmering flanks of the erstwhile ocean liner and a tear came to the corner of her eye.

A marine band played on the poop.

Floodlights wafted the smokestacks.

Awnings of silver and gold creaked.

The wealthy, the famous, the drones and the butterflies land-lubbered themselves aboard.

Leonard and Shemerelda were greeted on the quarter deck by Governor Olsen and his lady wife.

Shag of white mane. Deep fiords of wrinkles on his cheeks.

"Leonard. So nice of you to come."

"It is a pleasure, Governor. A real pleasure."

Maelstrom of blue Nordic eyes.

Trolling tremble to the hand.

"Shemerelda, my dear young woman. How enticing. How entrancing."

"Thank you, Governor."

Dry chirrup from lady wife.

Leonard and Shemerelda entered the Van Tromp ballroom.

The cream of the cream of Rackham City society was out in force.

"You see the movie last night?"

"Nope."

"You didn't see the movie last night?"

"Nope."

"I seen the movie last night. It sure was good."

What a congregation of leeching. What a jamboree of boot-lick and toady. What a squantum of truckle and kowtow.

Politico and gangster. Film star and usurer. Author and plagiarist.

Big knobs and small knobs.

"Shemerelda, your beauty is almost saintly," said Mr Ikin, the composer.

"You look great, Shemerelda, just great," said Mr Stollmeyer, the noted attorney.

Claret glow of nose.
Patter of gossip.
Dolphin leap of scandal.
"I would be most honored, if you would consent to dance with me, Shemerelda," said Leonard.
"Ah," said Shemerelda.
And she opened her arms to her husband, and away to the chocolate-bitter tang of *alter Wien* they waltzed.
Leonard danced lightly.
His movements were graceful.
The smile on his face was radiant.
Why?
Ruin faced him.
Collapse.
Disgrace.
Yet he beamed. He nodded. He grinned.
Why, why?
"Leonard," said Shemerelda sharply.
"Yes, Shemerelda?" said Leonard.
"I am interested in your enterprises."
"How curious."
"Curious?"
Leonard twirled her round with a stiff pivot of his leg and an expansive sweep of the shoulder, and her long golden hair, unrestrained by clip or clasp, swirled and rippled.
"Curious, Shemerelda," said Leonard. "You see, never before have you asked me a question about my business affairs. Indeed, Shemerelda, never before have you asked me a question about myself."
"Ah," said Shemerelda.
Leonard delicately steered Shemerelda round the twin hulks of Admiral and Mrs Kolokof.
Fastidiously he avoided the tentacular arms of Mr Edwin Culpepper, the noted toxicologist, and the harpooning hips of his fiancée, Clovissa.
"Everything prospers, Shemerelda," said Leonard. "And presently you shall see why."
The music stopped.
Shemerelda excused herself from Leonard's presence and made her way aloft to the open boat deck.
She leaned on the rail in the lee of a buxom lifeboat.

Behind her the city snarled and snarkled.

Ahead the river danced at the stars.

And then like the first crash of the storm-flung wave it hit her.

Mirakel.

Mirakel, Mirakel, Mirakel.

His memory hit her so forcefully she had to clutch tight to the rail.

For three whole days she had been empty of him.

Not a thought of him.

Not a whisper.

Why?

Why, why?

Now he was overpowering her, weakening her limbs, pounding her heart, pumping her veins, flooding the sweet juices of her body.

Mirakel, Mirakel, Mirakel.

He had tried to kill Leonard.

Why, why?

Where was he?

Mr Van Strjden knew.

Why, why?

Mirakel, Mirakel, Mirakel.

What mysteries clothed that knot-taut, nut-brown body?

That body!

The rolling breakers of his thighs.

The dip and plunge of his prow.

Mirakel, Mirakel, Mirakel.

"Shemerelda."

She turned sharply.

Standing behind her was the incredibly beautiful H. H. Washbrook.

He smiled his incredibly beautiful smile.

"All alone?"

She nodded.

The salt night air wafted in from the unseen husky ocean, and she began to shiver.

H. H. Washbrook took off the incredibly beautiful jacket of his white tuxedo and placed it round her shoulders.

Without speaking he clasped her in his arms.

She burrowed her head into his chest.

He began to stroke her long golden hair.

"Such a beautiful vessel," he said.

Shemerelda nodded.

Were these the arms that had broken the body of Rogan Shieff?

"Beautiful ships are like beautiful women."

She nodded.

Were these the hands which had snapped a neck?

"It is sinful when they are not used for their proper purpose."

She nodded.

Was this the chest which housed a heart so cold that murder could be done?

"I sailed on this ship once," said the incredibly beautiful H. H. Washbrook.

She pressed her thighs into him and rolled her hips softly.

"We sailed from the Baltic. How exquisite the green copper cupolas of old Stockholm. How still the waters of the archipelago. The captain wore a monocle. We sailed past icebergs and petrels fluttered in our wake. There was a grand ball every night. Beautiful women with long slim fingers and bold eyes. Such beautiful women. How they sighed. My word, how they sighed."

She sighed.

And as he held her in his incredibly beautiful arms he told her of other voyages.

He told her of schoonering the South Sea isles.

He told her of slooping the mist-bound Hebrides.

He told her of clippers and barques.

He told her of great liners ghosting through the Newfoundland Banks, weaving phosphorus wakes off Arab shores, plundering the waves of wild cat seas.

And silently out of the darkness a yacht, white and cool as an egret, slipped alongside the liner.

Ropes were thrown.

Ropes were secured.

Passengers whooped aboard.

"Our friend, Mr Van Strjden," said H. H. Washbrook.

And then very quietly he slipped his incredibly beautiful hands inside Shemerelda's dress and placed them on her breasts.

Hawsers quivered.

Mooring ropes strained.

How her body fought to free itself.

How it ached and yearned for the wild seas of abandoned passion and the still tropic waters of sated bliss.

The incredibly beautiful H. H. Washbrook held his hands on her breasts for quite a while.

Then he removed them and said:

"Shall we dance?"

"Thank you," said Shemerelda.

They danced to tango and rhumba.

They waltzed.

The crowds parted and stood back to watch them.

What an incredibly beautiful dancer he was.

How fluent. How masterful.

How sublime.

It was in the middle of a slow fox-trot that they were excused by Mr Van Strjden.

"I wonder, if you would be gracious enough, Mr Washbrook?" he said.

"Certainly," said the incredibly beautiful H. H. Washbrook.

And, touching with his lips the coolness of the palms of the hands which had held Shemerelda's breasts, he departed.

Mr Van Strjden smiled and nodded.

He shuffled Shemerelda round the ballroom.

He stood on her toe and giggled.

He backed into the rump of the celebrated poetess and scholar, Miss Wilhemina Cotton.

He tripped over the train of the distinguished hostess and light contralto, Miss Micaela Rubenstein.

"How I detest dancing, Shemerelda," he said.

"So I can see, Mr Van Strjden," said Shemerelda.

She looked up to the balcony and saw Laverne Van Strjden gazing down on them.

She waved to her.

Laverne Van Strjden nodded and downed her glass of scotch in a gulp and gurgle.

Her minute husband pressed himself into Shemerelda's body.

He grunted.

"Shemerelda," he said.

"Yes?"

"I am now prepared to reveal certain facts I have at my disposal concerning our mutual acquaintance, Mirakel."

Mirakel, Mirakel, Mirakel.

She felt faint with desire.

Her legs weakened.

She clung hold of Mr Van Strjden to keep her body upright.

He grunted.

"Beautiful, Shemerelda. Beautiful," he said. "But, please, I beg you, try to be a little more discreet."

Mirakel, Mirakel.

The pump and thrust of the trombone's slide.

The straddle of the cello.

The climactic clash of cymbal.

"Tomorrow, Shemerelda," said Mr Van Strjden as the dancers prepared to leave the floor. "Tomorrow you will present yourself at my apartment at Ocean Heights. There I shall reveal to you the whereabouts of Mirakel. And there, Shemerelda, you and I shall become lovers."

He smiled.

He nodded.

He squeezed her hand as he led her off the dance floor.

"*Bis Morgen*," he said, and he dappered away in a penguin pitter pat of dancing pumps.

Before Shemerelda could move she was grasped by the arm.

Grid iron fingers. Metallic wrist.

It was Laverne Van Strjden.

"Okay, honey. This way," she said and she pulled Shemerelda out of the ballroom.

Shemerelda did not resist as she was led firmly and swiftly across the placid carpets of the lounge ensnarled with its skerries of revellers and out onto the main deck.

Darkness inked by scudding cloud.

Grease of rain on planking.

Wraith-white glide of lonesome gull.

"Okay, honey," said Laverne Van Strjden. "Shoot."

"I beg your pardon, Laverne?" said Shemerelda.

"You slut. You stinking whore."

Laverne Van Strjden, snarling and spitting with rage, waved her purse above her head.

She took two steps towards Shemerelda.
She stumbled.
She swayed.
She lurched backwards into the rail of the liner.
"Laverne."
"Don't you 'Laverne' me, you crummy broad with your sticky-out nipples and your icebox crutch."
"Laverne. Please."
"Get yourself a lover, I said. Sure I did. So you got yourself a lover. Sure you did. My husband."
"What?"
"Don't come the innocent with me, baby. I seen you, kid. I seen you. Dancing cheek to cheek. Clinging to him. Sticking your tits in his nose."
"Laverne, you've got it . . ."
"Shut up, you bitch."
Laverne Van Strjden opened her purse and took out a Bamberg leather drinking flask.
She tilted it to her mouth and drank deeply.
She wiped her hand across her mouth and spat upon the deck.
"Bitch, bitch," she screamed.
Shemerelda watched as she staggered again, grasped at the rail and fell to her knees.
Draggles of hair across her brow.
Whinnies of rouge across her cheeks.
Mottled arms.
"Why my husband? Why steal him from me? Why shit on my life?"
"Your husband is not my lover, Laverne."
"What do you want a lover for anyways? You got everything a dame could desire. You gotta rich husband. You gotta beautiful home. You got wealth. You got beauty. You got happiness. What do you want a lover for?"
"But, Laverne, you yourself told me to get a lover. You yourself have had many lovers."
"No, I ain't, kid."
"What?"
She grappled with the rail and heaved herself to her feet.
She swayed slowly from side to side.
"I never had no lovers. Look at me. Who would want me? A

beat-up old broad with a long nose, sharp teeth and spikey elbows. All I got is big tits. All I got is a vivid imagination. Shemerelda, I never had no lovers. All those stories I told you? Lies. The Argentinian groom? The veterinarian? The personal bodyguard with the biggest . . ."

Bleakness flooded uncontrollably into the most secure and sheltered harbors of Shemerelda's soul.

Crumpled were the barriers.

Shattered the breakwaters.

Cast asunder the groynes, breached the sluices and the dykes.

". . . not a one. Not a single, stinking goddam one. And now you're going to take my husband from me. Sure you are. Sure you are. Bitch. Whore. Bitch. Bitch."

Laverne Van Strjden clutched at her throat.

Her chest convulsed.

Her cheeks expanded.

She turned, leaned over the rail and retched and retched.

And retched.

Shemerelda fled.

Hair streaming behind her, she raced along the deck.

Blindly she fought her way through the carousers as she elbowed her way to the gangway.

"Shemerelda! Shemerelda, my dear, what on earth is the matter with you?"

Leonard!

Plump and balding and smug as well.

"Take me home, Leonard. Take me home. Please. Please, I beg you."

"But, Shemerelda, the night is still young. There is still so much enjoyment to be had."

Shemerelda looked at him.

She looked at him hard.

And then she spat right into his face.

A long slow smile of satisfaction sidled over Leonard's features as he watched his wife hurry down the gangway, hail a cab from the quayside and speed off into the night.

chapter forty-one

Oh, bleakness.
Oh, despair.
The flood gates open.
In the back seat of the taxi cab Shemerelda sobs uncontrollably.
Tears spurt and cascade from her eyes.
Her whole body is wracked.
Tomorrow she must surrender her body.
The worm acrawl in the dry-husked bud.
This very night she felt the spears and thrusts of lust as incredibly beautiful hands cupped and caressed her breasts.
The serpent rampant in the fig-fresh gape.
Oh, misery.
Oh, bile-black wretchedness.
Gone is the icy calm.
Gone is the soul's deep stillness.
Gone is serenity.
Shemerelda surrenders to her grief.
Mirakel, Mirakel, Mirakel.
The cab speeds on past guttered rodent and spattered bird.
Its engine drums.
Its tyres thrum.
The tears do not subside as the cab skids to a halt on the gravel pathway.
They blind her eyes as she fumbles with her purse and the fawning dollar bills.
She stumbles.
She begins to fall.
Two strong arms reach out and hold her.
They hold her tightly.
"Mirakel," she gasps. "Mirakel, Mirakel, Mirakel."
The voice is deep and strong.
"Shemerelda."

chapter forty-two

"Are you ready, Shemerelda?"
"Yes."
"Come with me."
"Yes."
"I will take you away from here."
"Yes."
"We will live together."
"Yes."
"We will be happy."
"Yes."
"Take my hand. It is dark. My car is waiting, Shemerelda."
"Yes."
"Are you happy?"
"Oh, yes. Yes, yes, yes."

chapter forty-three

Five days have passed since the Governor's Ball.

Where are they?

Shemerelda and Mirakel?

Let us take a trip in the prototype of Leonard's airship.

No need to fear.

The gondola beneath the gas bag is quite secure.

Wicker armchairs.

How nice.

Sit down.

Relax.

Ready?

Good.

We shall cast off.

Look out of the windows as the ship rises from its mast.

Look down at the curving arch of the Downey River.

See its wharves and its quays and the tugboats and the lighters and the rusting tramps and the ocean liners.

The motors throb.

Over the skyscrapers we creep, a fat snail in the sky, but we leave no trail.

See the leafy squares and the brownstone mansions.

See the scummy creeks entwined with fire-escapes and downfall pipes and hissed with steam.

See the coarse-chested apartment blocks.

See the park with its joggers and its tumbling dogs.

See the roller skaters.

Nice?

Sure it is.

Sure.

Swing and sway of gondola.

A scrotum in the sky.

But look.

Look hard.

A tiny square.
A cock-spired church.
Let us descend.
The square is stone-flagged.
There are wooden benches there.
The houses are tall and narrow.
There is a barber's shop and a candy store.
Look.
See that ochre-coated house with the window-boxes brimming blue?
See the open window and the gentle flap of drape?
Sure you do.
Sure.
Well, inside that room you will find Mirakel and Shemerelda.
But, please.
Remove your gaze forthwith.
They are engaged in business, upon which only the insensitive would wish to intrude.

chapter forty-four

In a simple vase in that simple room stood a single bough.

It was a bough from the Tozer tree.

The buds were tightly shut.

Enwaxed.

But as Shemerelda and Mirakel explored the soft bowers and rampant arbors of love so did the buds strain at their sheaths.

So did the sap rise.

So did the leaves unfurl and the veins swell deep and purple.

"I love you, Mirakel.

"I adore you."

The bed was downy soft.

"Do that to me, Mirakel.

"Arrh.

"And that.

"Arrh.

"Again.

"Arrrh.

"Again, again, again.

"Arrrh."

The closet creaked.

It had handles of brass.

"Let me do this, Mirakel.

"Arrh.

"And this.

"Arrh.

"Again.

"Arrh.

"Again, again, again.

"Arrrrrh."

There was a chesterfield.

They made love on it.

"Now, Mirakel.

"Now, now, now.

"Arrrrh."

The scent of the gilly flowers wafted in from the window-box.

Sweet scents.

Sensuous scents.

"I love you, I love you, I love you.

"Arrrh."

There was a low chest of drawers with a pinewood mirror on it.

"I can see us, Mirakel.

"Look.

"Look at us.

"Look, look, look.

"Arrrh."

There was a deep-piled carpet.

They made love on it.

"Arrrh."

The walls were white.

The ceiling was white.

The drapes were the color of the spring blossoms of the Tozer tree.

"I love you, Mirakel.

"I love you, I love you, I love you.

"Arrrrrrrh."

chapter forty-five

"Mirakel?"

"Yes, Shemerelda?"

"Tell me something of yourself."

It was mid-afternoon.

All morning they had made love.

They had slept through noon.

Now they lay together in bed and drank throaty wine.

"I was born poor."

"Yes."

"My parents lived in a shack on the side of a mountain."

"Yes."

"In the winter we froze. In the summer we gasped from the heat.

"The spring was good.

"We had sheep with fat tails.

"We had dogs that killed wild birds.

"We had one room.

"The window was small to keep in the heat in winter and to keep out the heat in summer. We had a table and two chairs. My mother died when I was six. My father was sent to prison for stealing his neighbour's sheep. The landlord came to our shack with men and guns. They drove me and my five brothers off the land. The men beat us over our backs with the butts of their guns. We went to the town. We lived in the sewers. We stole from houses. We robbed people in the streets. The war came, and we returned to the mountains. We fought the enemy. I killed a soldier. He had fair hair, and he wore rimless spectacles. He went down on his knees and pleaded with me. I thrust a bayonet through his throat. The war ended. I had money. Gold. I returned to the city. I took the boat to the mainland. I lived in a grand apartment in a large square with a cathedral and fat pigeons. I had grand clothes. I had grand ladies.

"I had to leave my country.

"There was a revolution.

"I travelled the world.

"I made a living.

"I cut timber. I sheared sheep. I washed dishes. I heaved coal.

"I lived in hovels. I lived under bridges. I lived in tents of goatskin. I lived with black native women. I lived with soft-eyed Asiatic women. I lived with smokey-thighed women.

"I came to this country.

"I met your husband.

"I met you."

Every morning Mirakel would kiss the sleeping Shemerelda on her eyes.

He would put on his clothes and leave the room.

Tightly closed were the buds of the Tozer tree.

When Shemerelda awoke, she would hear small children playing in the square.

The smell of the baker's shop.

The smell of spices.

The strop of the barber's leather.

The scratching yowl of violin.

The rumble of the El.

Mirakel would return with fresh bread and cheese and creamy white butter.

He would make strong black coffee on the ring in the bathroom.

They would breakfast in bed.

Then they would make love.

"Arrrh."

In the evening Mirakel would put on his clothes and leave the room.

He would lock the door behind him.

Shemerelda would kneel on the chesterfield and look out over the evening square.

People promenaded.

Dogs gamboled.

Snuff-coloured wine sparkled.

That fat priest came out of the cock-spired church and lit up his bent stem pipe with the silver band.

He placed the spent matches in the brim of his black fedora.
Mirakel would return and take off his clothes.
They would lie in bed together and drink wine.
And then as darkness fell they would make love.

"Mirakel?"
"Yes, Shemerelda?"
"What are we going to do?"
"What do you want to do, Shemerelda?"
"I want to be with you, Mirakel.
"For ever and ever.
"I want us to have children.
"I want a small dry house.
"I want it to overlook gentle hills."
"That is what I want, too, Shemerelda."
"Mirakel?"
"Yes, Shemerelda?"
"I have money, you know. I am exceedingly wealthy."
"I know."
"It is all for you, Mirakel. Take it. Make us happy with it."
"We do not need your money, Shemerelda. We are happy without it. We will never use your money."
"Oh, Mirakel, Mirakel, I love you.
"I adore you.
"Do you love me?"
"Sleep, Shemerelda. Sleep."

chapter forty-six

Such happiness.

Such bliss.

Two lovers radiant.

The rich girl snatched from a life of idle emptiness.

The rich girl locked in the arms of her grizzled lover.

The lissom young body entwined round the knot-hard limbs of mystery and dark experience.

Ah yes.

Thus should all good love stories end.

But wait.

What do we see?

A plump and balding young man sits in his study.

He rubs his hands.

He smiles.

Why?

His wife has been snatched away from his weak and feeble grasp.

The rusting scimitar of the cuckold lies above his neck.

Yet he is happy.

Not a crinkle of care disturbs the calm of his brow.

Why?

Why, why, why?

And just look here.

Wow.

A minute man roosts high in his secret lair.

He lies at peace and at ease in the arms of his Goanese steward.

He nibbles at his black-pearl ears.

He nuzzles at his blue-black nipples.

He . . .

No, no, no.

Such sights are not for us.

Let us return to the cock-spired church and the snuff-coloured wine and the creamy croon of fat pigeons.

All is peace.

'Vulgar imprecation'

All is calm.
But is it?
Look.
There.
The atelier window in the pantiled roof.
Staring hard.
Staring intently.
A pair of incredibly beautiful eyes.
Oh shit.

chapter forty-seven

Mirakel returned to the room with long thin loaves of french bread batoned under his arm.

In a brown paper bag he had fresh olives, squat tomatoes, leather-parched goat cheese, plump bierwurst, kumquats, granadillas and nectarines.

From its wrapping of newspaper he took out a narrow-necked bottle, bulbous at the base.

Its liquid was limpid pink.

"Liqueur, Shemerelda.

"From my country.

"We shall celebrate."

Shemerelda, lying naked on the bed, watched him as he took off his clothes and folded them neatly on the cane-backed chair.

"Mirakel?"

"Yes, Shemerelda?"

"Why do you never take me out with you? Why do you always lock me in the room while you are away?"

"Danger, Shemerelda."

"Danger, Mirakel?"

"You must not be seen. Your husband has people searching for you. If they find you, they will take you away from me. We shall not see each other again. We shall never live in a small dry house. We shall have no children. We shall be unhappy."

Shemerelda drew him back to the bed.

She pulled him on top of her.

She took hold of him and guided him into her.

"Arrrh.

"Mirakel, Mirakel.

"Arrrh.

"Arrrh.

"I love you, Mirakel.

"I love you, darling."

chapter forty-eight

Oh, how the cream of the cream of Rackham City gossiped.

"You read the news about Shemerelda?"

"Nope."

"You didn't read the news about Shemerelda?"

"Nope."

"I read the news about Shemerelda. It sure was bad."

chapter forty-nine

They cried out in unison.

Mirakel's body shuddered.

Shemerelda convulsed.

Again.

And again.

They lay silently in each other's arms.

Their limbs gleamed.

"Mirakel?"

"Yes, Shemerelda?"

"When will we leave this room?"

"Very soon, Shemerelda.

"Documents are being prepared for us. Arrangements for travel are being made.

"Very soon they will be finished.

"And then we shall leave."

Shemerelda sighed.

"Mirakel?"

"Yes, Shemerelda?"

"Where shall we go to?"

"We shall go to my country, Shemerelda.

"We shall live in a land of gentle hills and tumbling streams.

"I shall build a house for you.

"You shall have a pony. There will be an orchard. We shall have two hives with lazy summer bees.

"There will be green shutters and red roses and deep blue gentians.

"At night we shall lie under the stars and we shall rub our bodies with honey.

"And we shall make long, sweet, lazy love."

Shemerelda coiled herself around her lover.

And as she looked down on him, and as his back arched to receive her, she whispered:

"I love you, Mirakel.

'Repeated blandishments'

"I love you, I love, I love you."
He smiled.
"Of course you do, Shemerelda."

chapter fifty

The fat cat sun arched its back round lazy pantiles and cock-spired church.

It cast warm purple shadows over flagstone, hosed and soused.

It sidled past gilly flower and Tozer bough and rubbed itself against the bodies of Mirakel and Shemerelda as they ate kumquat and goat cheese, olives and crisp french bread.

They drank throaty wine.

When they had finished, Mirakel put on his clothes.

"This is the last time I shall leave you, Shemerelda," he said.

"Oh, Mirakel, Mirakel."

"I am to finalise arrangements for our travel. I am to collect our documents."

"Take care, Mirakel. Please take care, darling."

Mirakel smiled.

He kissed Shemerelda on the forehead.

"Good-bye," he said.

He did not turn round as he left the room.

The key turned in the lock.

His footsteps echoed on the romping wooden stairs.

Shemerelda ran to the window and watched him as he hurried across the square.

Purposeful stride.

Head hunched.

Looking neither to right nor left.

He disappeared in the cool cleft of alley beside the cock-spired church.

Shemerelda sighed.

She turned back to the interior of the room.

Crumbs of french bread littered the bed.

She picked up the newspaper.

She commenced to brush the crumbs into it.

And then she saw the headline.

'Considerable shock'

Backwards she reeled.
Sickening thud in guts.
Bells clanging in mind.
Sirens wailing.
A long slow silent scream from deep within.
This is what she read:
"TOZER KIDNAP HEIRESS – FIVE MILLION DOLLAR RANSOM DEMAND".
She fell to the floor.
She clawed at the carpet.
She bit at it.
She wrenched at it.
At the top of her voice she screamed.
She screamed and she screamed and she screamed.

chapter fifty-one

Treachery.
Vile deceit.
Base duplicity.
The sated bees are frozen in their hives.
The tumbling stream is parched.
The house walls crumble.
All is dust.
All is ruin.
Shemerelda.
Oh, Shemerelda.

chapter fifty-two

When Mirakel entered the room, Shemerelda flung herself at him.

Scratching.

Spitting.

Biting.

He grappled with her.

"Shemerelda? Shemerelda?"

She scored a great searing gash down his cheek.

She bit his chest.

She hammered with her fists at his groin.

He flung her back across the bed.

He stood over her, panting, clenching his knuckles.

"Shemerelda, what is the matter with you?"

She picked up the empty bottle of wine, broke off the neck and launched herself at him once more.

He deflected the bottle's blow with his forearm.

Blood spurted at the ceiling and spattered in the golden silk of Shemerelda's hair.

She ducked under his grasp and rammed the broken bottle straight at his eyes.

He brought up his fist.

Sharp.

Swift.

It struck Shemerelda's wrist.

The bottle flew from her grasp.

It shattered into fragments against the wall.

She screamed, and she hurled herself at him, nails bared, teeth hissing.

He struck her.

He struck her with the flat of his hand.

Hard.

Against her cheek.

She flew backwards through the air and crashed into the

cane-backed chair and struck her head against the leg of the dresser.

She rolled over onto her stomach.

And then after a while she hunched herself into a soft quivering ball and whimpered.

Mirakel stood motionless in the centre of the room.

Blood streamed down his cheek.

Blood oozed from his forearm.

The marks of teeth pocked his neck and his chest.

And then on the bed he saw the newspaper.

He read it slowly.

He picked it up.

He walked towards Shemerelda.

He stood above her.

With the toe of his shoe he rolled her over onto her back.

She looked up at him with eyes stricken by terror.

"This?" he said holding up the newspaper.

She nodded.

"I see."

A snarl of a smile came to his lips.

"So," he said. "So."

Shemerelda cowered.

His eyes narrowed.

His jaw contorted.

"So there we are, Shemerelda," he said. "There we are."

He crumpled up the newspaper and let it drop to the floor.

And then with a sudden movement he took Shemerelda by the arm and hoisted her to her feet.

He dragged her to the bed.

She did not resist.

She did not whimper.

Oh, brave Shemerelda.

What courage.

Not a flinch as he placed his hands beneath the pit of her arms.

Not a tremble as he drew her up to the level of his narrowed eyes.

He stared at her.

She felt the pressure of his fingers as he clamped them into the bones of her shoulders.

Slowly he forced her backwards.

'Very tightly closed eyes'

She closed her eyes.
Tight.
Tight.

chapter fifty-three

That's it then.

Farewell, Shemerelda

All over.

Kaput.

For God's sake, whatever happened to happy endings?

What happened to the days when virtue triumphed and evil was vanquished?

Why all this misery?

Why all this despondency?

Isn't life bad enough without . . .

Hold on.

Not so hasty.

Mirakel is about to speak.

chapter fifty-four

"It is not true, Shemerelda."

She opened her eyes.

"I tell you, what is written in the newspaper is not true."

She screamed.

He struck her across the face once more.

Lightly this time.

And, lightly too, he laid her on the bed.

"Listen to me.

"Do not interrupt.

"I shall tell you all.

"One day I received a call.

"I was to meet a man.

"I drove to Beecher's Quay.

"He was waiting for me at the Smugglers' Inn.

"It was your husband.

"He had a proposition.

"I was to kidnap his wife. I was to demand five million dollars ransom. The money would be paid from his wife's resources. I was to keep fifty thousand dollars. He was to keep the rest. Then I was to murder his wife.

"He invited me to a ball at his house.

"I was to be introduced to his wife.

"I met her.

"I met you, Shemerelda.

"And at once I fell in love with you.

"I tried to pull out of the deal.

"It was not possible.

"Money had been paid.

"I am an honorable man.

"I told your husband's assistant of the plot. He said he would help. He used the information to try to make you take him as your lover. I intended to kill him. Someone got there first.

"I tried to kill your husband.
"But instead I killed your chauffeur.
"I tried to flee the country.
"I couldn't.
"I loved you Shemerelda. I craved for you. I wanted you. I had to stay.
"Then someone else approached me.
"I was taken to an apartment building.
"It had a glass-floored lobby and a Goanese steward. I was told I had to keep my contract. I was told I would be killed, if I did not.
"So I planned.
"I plotted.
"I waited for you at your home.
"You came home from the Governor's Ball alone.
"I took you away.
"I took you to this room.
"We made love.
"We were happy.
"Tonight I was to take you away.
"Tonight we were to flee.
"You and I.
"Just you and I, Shemerelda.
"Away from evil.
"Away from danger.
"Away from treachery.
"Away from corruption.
"We were to flee to happiness.
"And now I see this paper.
"It is not true, Shemerelda.
"It is not true.
"Your husband has invented the demand.
"I have not made it.
"I swear it.
"Your husband has invented the story to cover himself.
"He will send men for us.
"They will find us.
"They will kill me.
"You will be alone, Shemerelda.
"All alone."
He looked down on her.

'Repeated questions'

Her eyes did not blink.
Her body did not move.
"Do you believe me, Shemerelda?"
Not a motion to her head.
Not a sound from her voice.
"You must believe me.
"You have to believe me.
"Do you, do you, do you?
"Do you believe me, Shemerelda?"

chapter fifty-five

You must believe him, Shemerelda.
You must.
You must.
Go on.
Tell him you believe him.

chapter fifty-six

Very slowly Shemerelda turned her head away from Mirakel.

Very slowly she raised her arm.

Silently she pointed at the vase on the dresser.

Silently they watched the Tozer bud break through its waxy sheath and burst into a shimmering black blossom.

She turned to him.

"I believe you, Mirakel," she said.

"Shemerelda, I love you," he cried.

He moved towards her, ripping at his shirt, kicking off his shoes, chest heaving, eyes cascading with tears.

And at that moment the door burst open.

A pistol was pointed at their heads.

It was held by a pair of incredibly beautiful hands.

chapter fifty-seven

The incredibly beautiful H. H. Washbrook was followed into the room by two people.

Leonard and Mr Van Strjden.

The minute bon vivant and epicure smiled.

"Good afternoon, Shemerelda," he said.

Silence.

Pump of heart.

Coo of pigeon.

Trill of children's laughter.

"We have found your wife for you, Leonard," he said.

Quiver of plump cheek.

Mop of brow.

Tremble of damp, plump hand.

"How clever of Mr Washbrook," said Mr Van Strjden. "And how careless of our friend, Mirakel."

Clang of cock-spired church clock.

Scratch of violin.

Slap of barber's strop.

Slam of door.

Mr Van Strjden nodded.

He smiled.

"Well then, Mr Washbrook," he said. "Let us take our victims to their fate."

chapter fifty-eight

Night
A yacht.
White.
Frail flimses of sea fret.
Black.
Slack tide.
In the saloon of the yacht sit Mr Van Strjden, Leonard, Shemerelda, Mirakel and the incredibly beautiful H. H. Washbrook.
Muffled lamps.
Dull glow of brass.
Drift of carpet.
Mr Van Strjden speaks.
"It is time for me to explain, Shemerelda.
"Your husband is in my debt.
"He has been for a considerable time.
"How to redeem that debt?
"Kidnap.
"It was I who suggested he arrange for your kidnap.
"He did.
"Typically he flunked it."
Leonard perspires.
His face flushes pink.
His eyes dart.
"His personal assistant made an intervention.
"He had to be eliminated.
"Unfortunate.
"But it gave me an idea, Shemerelda.
"If he could bring influence to bear on you to compel you to become his lover, so could I.
"I did."
He pauses.

He smiles.
He taps off the ash from his Cavereglio cigar.
"Did you know that, Leonard?"
Silence.
Sharply.
"I asked you, Leonard, if you knew."
Pause.
Leonard licks his drip lips.
He whispers:
"No."
Mr Van Strjden nods.
He smiles.
"Wickedness is so delectable, is it not?
"I have dedicated my life to it."
He laughs.
It chills.
Shemerelda is impassive.
So, too, is Mirakel.
Leonard shivers.
The incredibly beautiful H. H. Washbrook narrows his incredibly beautiful eyes.
Mr Van Strjden speaks.
"And now more wickedness is in order, I think.
"Shemerelda, my dear.
"Mirakel.
"It is time for you to die."
The choke of a soblet from Leonard.
Mr Van Strjden turns to him.
"You don't agree, Leonard?"
Silence.
Sharply.
"Leonard!
"An answer, if you please."
A pause.
Leonard speaks.
"I agree."
"How glad I am to hear it, Leonard," says Mr Van Strjden, and he stubs out his Cavereglio cigar in an ashtray of Suk Cha Ho porcelain.
Water laps the skirts of the yacht.
Its reflection ripples on the ceiling.

Mr Van Strjden turns to the incredibly beautiful H. H. Washbrook.

"Mr Washbrook, over to you, my dear chap.

"I trust you have devised a suitable death for our two precious friends."

The incredibly beautiful H. H. Washbrook turns to Shemerelda.

"Oh yes," he says. "I have prescribed an incredibly beautiful death."

chapter fifty-nine

Shemerelda and Mirakel are led to their deaths.

The venue?

Brandon Fields.

Three airships nod gently at their masts.

One red.

One blue.

One silver-gray.

Prototypes.

The incredibly beautiful H. H. Washbrook alights from the black limousine with the silver condor's head statuette.

He helps out Shemerelda.

Leonard, Mirakel and Mr Van Strjden alight, too.

Mr Van Strjden smiles.

Leonard shifts from foot to foot.

The incredibly beautiful H. H. Washbrook speaks.

"One red airship.

"One blue airship.

"One for you, Mrs Tozer.

"One for you, Mirakel.

"The controls are simple.

"You will find them easy to fly.

"You will find it a most enjoyable experience, in fact.

"There is one drawback.

"One airship is designed to blow up after five minutes in the air.

"Extremely elegant, don't you think?"

He smiles his incredibly beautiful smile.

Mr Van Strjden claps his hands with delight.

"And the silver-gray airship?" he says.

"That, my dear sir, will be our grandstand," says the incredibly beautiful H. H. Washbrook. "You, Mr Tozer and myself, shall take to the air in it. And from it we shall see the whole wondrous panoply of violent death."

Mr Van Strjden laughs.

"My congratulations, Mr Washbrook," he says.

"An extremely elegant death.

"I have but one query.

"Yes?" says the incredibly beautiful H. H. Washbrook.

"There will be one survivor?"

"Yes."

"What will be the fate of that survivor?"

The incredibly beautiful H. H. Washbrook smiles his incredibly beautiful smile once more.

"The survivor will be mine to do with as I please," he says. "The survivor will be my fee for the project I have undertaken on your behalf."

He turns to Shemerelda.

"Let us hope, my dear Mrs Tozer, that the survivor is you."

chapter sixty

The coin is tossed.

Heads for the red airship.

Tails for the blue airship.

Heads.

The red airship is for Shemerelda.

Which airship contains the lethal explosion?

Only the incredibly beautiful H. H. Washbrook knows.

Oh, the bravery of it all.

The cool courage of Shemerelda as she enters the lift at the foot of the mast.

The unflinching fortitude as she is locked into the control gondola of the red airship.

Magnificent.

Let piano chords crash in praise.

Let brass ring out in exultation.

Let strings soar and tumble in glittering hallelujahs.

No need to mop our eyes.

No distress.

This is a brave sight.

This is a noble prospect as the red airship and the blue airship nudge away from their masts and nose out into the clear blue skies of dawn.

Away and away they float, motors throbbing, prows bowing and curtseying.

And in their wake the snarling grin of the silver-gray airship and the snicker of its motors.

No tears.

Please.

Let us be uplifted and inspired.

Let us resolve to lead better lives.

Be loving to our spouses, considerate to our servants, kind to dumb animals.

Let us remember this sight to our dying day.

chapter sixty-one

One minute gone.

Shemerelda grappled with the controls of the airship.

She could steer it to the right.

She could steer it to the left.

But downwards?

No.

The control refused to budge.

Over the Downey River.

Tugs, lighters, tramps, tankers and ocean liners.

High roosts of apartment blocks.

Joggers in the park.

Dutch fort.

Wharehouse and wharf.

The sparkle of the crab-fested ocean.

Two minutes gone.

The blue airship hove into view on her left.

Mirakel.

Mirakel, Mirakel, Mirakel.

Let it be her airship which exploded.

Let her shattered body be taken to the gentle hills of her childhood.

Let it be buried in a warm dry plot between her grandfather and his old cork leg.

Let Mirakel live.

Let him return to the country of his birth.

Let him wander the mountains, hunt wild boar, gather sensuous herbs, thrill to the lammergeier's stoop.

Let him find himself a loving woman with smouldering brown eyes, plump breasts, wide hips and stout legs.

Let him live.

Please, let him live.

Three minutes gone.

The blue airship came nearer.

So close she could see Mirakel.

He beckoned to her.

Urgently.

Why?

Why, why, why?

In an instant she realised.

The crackling waves of telepathy flooded over her, illuminated her whole being, lit up her mind in a blinding rose-red hue.

Yes, yes, she understood.

She and Mirakel would die together.

Side by side their airships would float.

Whichever one exploded, would inevitably conflagrate the other to its doom.

They would die together.

Mirakel, oh, Mirakel.

Their airships touched timidly, tenderly.

Two lovers innocent and fresh.

Two lovers stroking each other's flanks.

Two lovers embarking on eternal passion.

She waved to him.

He waved to her.

Her eyes sparkled.

Bliss.

Death with her lover.

Happiness sublime.

Over the water meadows they floated.

Over glistening creeks, leaping dolphins, squat fishermen's cottages, slumbering mansions, shuttered clapboard houses, golden, rolling strands.

Together, together.

Four minutes gone.

One minute to blessed oblivion.

Her loins ached.

Her tongue coiled slowly over her lips.

Her body tingled.

How it yearned for the caresses of her lover.

Mirakel, Mirakel, Mirakel.

Locked forever in death's loving embrace.

Mirakel, I love you.

Mirakel, I adore you.

Arrrh.

And then suddenly..

A shadow.

Black.

Dark.

Brooding.

Menacing.

It cut out the sun to her right.

She turned.

Alongside her was the silver gray airship.

She saw the faces of Leonard, Mr Van Strjden and the incredibly beautiful H. H. Washbrook.

Closer and closer came the silver gray airship.

Her heart pumped.

What was wrong?

On the faces of Leonard and Mr Van Strjden panic.

Fear.

Rampant terror.

The window of the silver-gray airship's gondola opened.

The incredibly beautiful H. H. Washbrook began to climb out, pistol pointing at the heads of Leonard and Mr Van Strjden.

He turned to Shemerelda.

He paused.

He smiled his incredibly beautiful smile.

And then with one mighty leap he sprang towards the red airship.

Incredible.

Magnificent.

He clung hold of the mooring ropes of the red airship.

Hand over hand he climbed up them to the gondola.

His incredibly beautiful face appeared at the window.

He gesticulated.

Rapidly.

But calmly of course.

Shemerelda darted forwards and opened the window.

He scrambled in.

He brushed Shemerelda aside as he dashed to the control panel.

He took the joy stick in his hand and jerked it violently to the left.

The red airship heeled over.

Hard.

Locked to it was the blue airship.

Away they plummeted.

Down, down, down.

The incredibly beautiful H. H. Washbrook grappled with the controls.

Could he do it?

Could he stop their heedless fall?

Downwards, downwards, two airships plunging to their doom.

It was the shock waves of the explosion which stopped the vessels dead in their tracks.

It held them motionless.

Calm.

Still.

They were stable.

Upright.

Away to their right they saw the fireball of the silver-gray airship as it twisted and turned in the summer sky and then in a fiery gulp plunged to the ocean.

The incredibly beautiful H. H. Washbrook smiled.

"As I told you, Shemerelda," he said. "Only one man knew which airship contained the explosive device.

"A most elegant solution to our predicament, don't you think?"

And he moved across the gondola and waved to Mirakel with an incredibly beautiful arm.

chapter sixty-two

Hurrah.

A happy ending.

Virtue triumphs.

In the lower gardens of the vine-encrusted mansion the Tozer tree blooms.

Riotously.

Jet and black the blossoms.

In its shade sit Mirakel, Shemerelda and the incredibly beautiful H. H. Washbrook.

Laughter.

Joy unbounded.

Shemerelda takes Mirakel in her arms.

"Oh, Mirakel, Mirakel, let us make love."

"Yes, Shemerelda, yes."

"Yes, let us be wild with passion."

"Yes, Shemerelda, yes."

"Now, Mirakel, now."

"Yes, Shemerelda, yes."

The incredibly beautiful H. H. Washbrook rises to his incredibly beautiful feet.

"Please, my dear, please," he says. "Tomorrow is soon enough for that."

chapter sixty-three

Yes.

Yes.

What an incredibly beautiful ending.